GAIL RICHARDS

◆

A MATCH FOR THE FOOTMAN

Complete and Unabridged

LINFORD
Leicester

First published in Great Britain in 2019

First Linford Edition
published 2020

A catalogue record for this book is available
from the British Library.

ISBN 978–1–4448–4583–9

Published by
Ulverscroft Limited
Anstey, Leicestershire

Set by Words & Graphics Ltd.
Anstey, Leicestershire
Printed and bound in Great Britain by
T. J. International Ltd., Padstow, Cornwall

This book is printed on acid-free paper

A MATCH FOR THE FOOTMAN

It's 1844, and housemaid Emma's life of toil in Lewin Hall is brightened by the arrival of handsome new footman Thomas. When Emma is given an opportunity, along with Thomas and a few others, to work without supervision restoring a neglected house, they relish the freedom and responsibility. But malign influences are at work. As Emma fights to make sense of events, will she be able to protect everything she holds dear — and will her and Thomas's love survive all they have to face?

1

There. That was the last of the front steps clean and Emma could stand up and stretch. Only one more job before breakfast. She was ready for her porridge and tea.

Emma liked to rest her eyes for a moment by looking into the distance down the driveway to the iron gates beyond. They usually stood open so she could see to the hilly woodland opposite.

She didn't see the tall man standing by the steps and bumped into him as she stepped back.

'Oh, pardon, Miss,' he said, as flustered as she was.

Emma rubbed her eyes with the back of her hand. In her confusion she first thought it was William, the footman — but what would he be doing out at the front at this time of day? Had he been watching her work? And why would he call her Miss, when she'd known him since she started as a housemaid at Lewin Hall nearly five months earlier?

A look into his face showed her it wasn't him.

He was as tall and slim as William but his nose was smaller. His eyes were a deeper shade of brown and his hair lighter, with a stray lock falling over his forehead. She wondered if he knew. She had a strange urge to lift her hand and brush the wayward lock away.

William was plain and cheerful and his positive outlook had often lifted Emma's spirits — he reminded her of her brother, and he treated her like the sister he never had.

The newcomer reddened as he and Emma stood looking at one another. She wondered what he was seeing. Just an ordinary girl in a long black dress and white apron, not very tall, and plumper than he. She hoped her white collar and cuffs and cap were still clean and her dark hair wasn't escaping from the bun she'd scraped it back into before she'd started work two hours earlier.

'Hello,' she said finally.

He smiled and Emma felt a curious leaping in her chest. His mouth was wider than William's and there was something about those beautifully shaped lips that drew Emma. She lost all her appetite for breakfast.

'Hello,' he replied. Emma sat back down on the bottom step to hide the trembling in her legs.

*   *   *

Emma came hurtling down the back stairs and bumped into the kitchen maid, nearly knocking the poor girl over on the landing. It was only just gone eight o'clock and already it seemed to be a day for bumping into people. At least Emma knew young Ada well and they both laughed.

'I was coming up to tell you to hurry,'

Ada said. 'But if you hurried any more we'd both be at the bottom of the staircase.'

'Is Cook in a bad mood?' Emma asked. 'I just wanted to tidy myself up before I sat down to breakfast — she complained yesterday that I looked a mess.'

'Not really,' the kitchen maid replied. 'Everything's a bit of a flutter downstairs. There's been another robbery!' She turned to go back downstairs. 'I was just going to ask if Lily was on her way — I keep forgetting.'

'I know,' Emma said ruefully. 'She's been gone for nearly two months now and sometimes I'm still surprised not to see her in our room.'

The other maids were finishing their food and hurrying away from the long table in the servants' hall to begin their next task. Ada dolloped Emma out a bowl of porridge and some tea. The porridge was thick and sweet, the way Emma liked it.

As every morning, she spared a

thought for her younger sister and brothers, who may well be hungry at this moment. She was waiting for the day she would receive her wages and send them to her mother — or better still, take them — but it was over a month to her first payday.

'It's Eastbury Manor that's been robbed this time,' Cook said.

'What, in the night?' Emma asked.

The Manor was on the other side of the village. It felt as though the robberies were getting closer and closer. They'd started in other parts of the district, then some of the small businesses along the main thoroughfare between Lewin Hall and Eastbury Manor had also been targeted but now it seemed the big houses were also in danger. Emma knew any robbers wouldn't make their way up to the servants' rooms in the attic, but she felt uncomfortable for Lord and Lady Lewin.

'We don't know any details,' Cook said. 'Mrs Honey has gone down there to see if the housekeeper needs any help.'

That was kind of the Lewin Hall housekeeper, Emma thought. Mrs Honey was strict with her staff but had a good heart. Emma let her thoughts drift. She was certain Mrs Honey knew where Lily had gone but she refused to say anything.

William came in and sat down heavily at the table.

'What's the matter?' Emma asked, as Ada served him his breakfast.

'They've taken on another footman,' he said sulkily. 'Why do they need another footman?'

'That'll be good, though, won't it?' Emma asked. 'Having help? You were just saying the other day there wasn't always anyone to help lay the table.'

'They told me when I started there wasn't enough money for two of us. Then His Lordship met this man one day and just asked him to come and work here.' William stirred his porridge miserably. 'I'm worried they'll use me till this fellow gets here and then want to be rid of me.'

'They've got no reason,' Emma said.
He looked across the table at her.

'No,' he said. 'They haven't.' Then he got back to his porridge and soon Cook was bustling them all out and setting little Ada to washing the plates and pots — the second lot of a dozen times, Emma knew, during the course of a long day.

Emma dismissed her conjectures about her friend Lily, and thought instead of the tall young man with light brown hair. She felt that curious flutter again as she realised he might be coming to work with them. He'd asked for the butler and she'd directed him to the back door. He could have come for a job as footman. She felt sorry for William, but her life of toil suddenly started to look brighter.

*　*　*

'Emma, you and me are cleaning Lady Lewin's bedchamber,' another maid, Kitty, said to her later. 'Mrs Honey has

7

taken Jean and Connie to the Manor to help.'

'All right,' Emma said. She followed Kitty up the back staircase to their employers' rooms.

Kitty stopped suddenly. 'Would you mind if I ran down quickly to see Eric?' she said. 'I'll only be a minute.'

Emma knew that Kitty was in love with Eric, one of the under-gardeners, and the two took every chance they could to talk.

Emma didn't often enter the corridor with the bedchambers in, and never on her own. She was startled by a swish of skirts alerting her to the presence of someone else.

Her Ladyship had come out of her daughter's bedchamber. All of their Lordships' other children had married and left home; Miss Elizabeth was the only one remaining at Lewin Hall. Her Ladyship closed the door behind her and was now walking towards Emma.

Emma lowered her eyes and pressed herself into the wall, as she'd been told to do. The woman walked past without seeming to see her. At the last minute Emma looked up and received an impression of creamy-white skin and a green and silver pendant around her neck. Jewellery, at ten o'clock in the morning! And Lady Lewin smelled of flowers.

Emma waited until she was out of sight before she moved again. Had Her Ladyship pretended not to see her, or was Emma really so beneath notice she actually didn't register her existence? Emma and Lily had sometimes wondered this in their night-time conversations before sleep overtook them. Emma was inclined to think it was all a pretence.

Lying in the hard beds in the tiny attic room, they'd often talked of the future. Lily's wish was for love and security and a family of her own, and Emma was certain that would be her only reason for leaving Lewin House.

'I'm sure there's a handsome valet each waiting for us somewhere,' Lily would say.

'Or a gardener,' Emma suggested.

9

'Anyway I'm sure in your case it will happen. You're so sweet and pretty no man could resist you.'

But now Emma came to think about it, Lily hadn't seemed so happy before she left just after Easter. They hadn't had one of their conversations about the future for a couple of weeks.

Lily had been fine and then she'd gone quiet. And then she had disappeared.

She'd left her uniform and taken her most treasured possession, a lock of hair that had belonged to the mother she had never known. They had given it to her in the orphanage when she'd left, aged eight, to come and work as a scullery maid at Lewin Hall.

'Lily has found another place,' Mrs Honey said to everyone at the Hall. 'She needed to take it up without delay.' And to Emma, 'It's a step up for her.'

That didn't explain why Lily went without saying anything. She didn't want another place. She wanted a handsome valet, like Emma.

Or footman, Emma thought now.

⋆   ⋆   ⋆

Emma sat on for a while in the servants' hall after Kitty and the others had gone to bed. She was very tired and it had been a long day, but she didn't like going to her room knowing Lily would not be there.

Eventually she stood up and walked along the corridor where the bells used by the family and visitors to call for the servants were ranged high up in a row, then past the kitchen and towards the stairs. She realised she could hear voices.

Mrs Honey, the housekeeper, was talking to someone in her parlour. She assumed it was the butler Mrs Honey was talking to, but with a shock she realised from the tone that it must be Lady Lewin. Her Ladyship downstairs in the housekeeper's parlour — that was unheard of!

The door was slightly open and the

two must have thought everyone had gone up, because they weren't lowering their voices. Emma may not have lingered even then — she didn't feel like listening to anyone else's secrets tonight — but she thought she heard the word 'Lily'.

'It's very worrying but I'm sure we're safe here,' Her Ladyship said. 'What was the woman's name again?' It sounded as though she was right by the door now so Emma slipped quickly past, not wanting to be caught listening.

'Mary Ann,' Mrs Honey said. 'She seems to know everything that goes on, that's all.'

'You don't think she's involved?'

'It's most unlikely.'

'Can you find out?' Lady Lewin opened the door and Emma moved further away.

She still managed to hear Mrs Honey answer, 'I'll try.'

So who was Mary Ann and exactly what did she know? About the robberies, or where Lily was?

As she prepared for sleep Emma, for the first time, had a real handsome man to dream about, not just an imaginary one. But she had no Lily to share her hopes with.

2

William came and sat with Emma in the servants' hall the next night.

'You're still worried about Lily, aren't you?' he asked. 'I am, too. Going to another place without saying anything seems so unlike her.'

'Not so much worried,' she answered. 'More sad she couldn't tell me where she was going.'

'You don't think she was . . . taken, then?'

'I'm sure she went of her own free will. She took the lock of her mother's hair.'

'Ah,' William said, the concern on his face clearing. 'She planned it, then.'

'I'm certain of it,' Emma said. She wished they had talked of it earlier so she could have reassured him. 'I just wish she had told me.'

'She talked to you, didn't she?' he

asked. 'Did she have a . . . a follower — do you know?'

'No. She would have said.'

After she'd said that, Emma doubted herself. She would have said, surely? But thinking about when Lily stopped talking she began to wonder.

'There was the lad who delivered the butter. She chatted to him, didn't she?' William asked.

'Lily chatted to everyone,' Emma said.

William laughed. 'You may be right.' He paused. 'I've a problem of my own right now too.'

'Is the new footman coming?'

'Yes, when his employer lets him go.' William sighed. 'But when I went out with His Lordship last week they gave me my dinner downstairs and the second footman was talking about leaving to do something else because he wasn't good-looking and wouldn't get any further.'

'What did he mean?' Emma asked.

'They like handsome footmen, Emma,' William said. 'It makes them look better.' He paused as if thinking it over. 'I was surprised, to be honest. I didn't think they even saw us. It's as though you don't exist except as a statue that does their bidding and passes the food to them.'

'There you are,' Emma said. 'Why would they care so long as you do the work well?'

'But they do care, according to this chap. He was a funny-looking devil, it's true, but he spoke to me as though I was in the same boat as him. Suppose the new fellow's handsome?'

'You're handsome, William,' Emma exclaimed.

It wasn't quite true and they both knew it, but she wanted to cheer him up. It would be better if he welcomed the new footman as they would have to work closely together. Besides, she had the image of the likely one firmly etched in her mind and couldn't wait for him to start at the Hall.

★　★　★

16

There was a walled space just a few steps from the back door where Emma liked to escape to whenever she could — if she had a minute for a breath of air and if Cook would let her go through.

It was known as the small garden. You had to go past the kitchen garden, where the smells of the herbs were strong. Emma noticed the scents intensified as May turned to June. There was rosemary, dill and fennel for cooking, lavender to repel insects and bee balm for coughs and colds.

William sought her out there not long after their conversation. 'I spoke to the lad from the dairy,' he said. 'He remembers Lily but never knew her name and didn't even realise she'd disappeared.'

Emma nodded. 'Don't ever go without saying anything,' she entreated William.

He laughed, as if such a thing weren't even a possibility. 'If I had to go, I'd wait in the folly before I left the Hall,' he told her. 'Come and find me there before I disappear completely. But you'll have to promise to do the same.'

'Where and what is the folly?' she asked, laughing too. It sounded as though he was jesting.

'It's a building in the grounds that looks like a small castle,' William explained. 'There's nothing inside but a stone bench. There are four turrets with narrow stairs going up.' He made a movement with his hand of going up a winding staircase. 'There's supposed to be a good view of the grounds from the towers.'

'What's it for?' Emma asked.

'Nothing,' William told her. 'It's amusing for visitors, that's all. It's why it's called a folly.'

He led her around the edge of the small garden and through an open gate to the parkland beyond. Emma had never ventured this far into the grounds.

'You see that little copse up the hill there?' William said, pointing. 'If you go round it you'll see the towers further up the hill.'

Emma didn't know whether she'd have the courage to make her way up there on her own. By day there would be the chance of being stopped by someone from the family or one of the gardeners, and by night — well, it was dark out there and the nocturnal creatures made such strange noises.

'Promise?' William said.

She looked at his cheerful face. Surely nothing would happen that would cause either of them to have to go there.

'I promise,' she said.

She was comforted that William had made an attempt to trace Lily but, deep down, Emma didn't see how the two of them would be able to find her, especially if Mrs Honey were standing in their way. William had a little more freedom than she did, it was true, and could at least go out and question people like the boy who delivered the butter, but it made her think about the controlled life of serving staff and the limited choices they had. She began to admit to herself that if they didn't have the freedom to choose what they wore, when they ate or where they went, they would probably never have enough freedom to find out where Lily had gone.

★ ★ ★

Mrs Honey called Emma into her parlour a few days later.

'We're expecting a visitor,' she told Emma. 'I'd like you to look after the second-best bedchamber while he's here.'

'Yes, Mrs Honey,' Emma said. 'You want me to take the hot water up, like Lily used to do?'

The housekeeper nodded. 'And answer the bell. Mr Hardcastle will be arriving tomorrow and staying for a week.' She nodded to dismiss Emma. 'He shouldn't be any trouble,' she added.

Emma stayed where she was, standing in front of the seated housekeeper. That was an odd thing to say — as if some guests did cause trouble.

'Thank you, Emma.'

'Mrs Honey,' Emma suddenly blurted out. 'Where did Lily go?'

Mrs Honey looked away before she answered. 'Lily is all right,' she said. 'She'll be settled in her new place now and not wanting to look back.'

Mrs Honey turned back to her desk and Emma knew the conversation was over.

Mr Hardcastle arrived the next afternoon and Emma was called straight away to take him water for washing after his journey and before the evening meal with the family.

She knocked with some trepidation, not knowing what to expect, and a pleasant voice called for her to come in. Mr Hardcastle was tall, agreeable-looking and nicely dressed, and he came forward to take the water jug from her.

He smiled as he did so. 'Thank you, Emma.'

She left, deeply relieved. That wasn't so bad. Should she have curtsied? Probably not — he was only a Mr after all.

He deserved a curtsey out of respect, though. He'd bothered to learn her name and had eased her of her burden as soon as he could. She liked him already.

He didn't have twinkling brown eyes or a lock of hair falling onto his forehead, it was true, but he wasn't going to make her life difficult while he was here and for that Emma was grateful.

'Who is this Mr Hardcastle?' she asked Kitty one day just before the servants' evening meal.

'He's an attorney helping His Lordship sort out his land affairs,' Kitty said. 'Though he seems to be spending more time with Miss Elizabeth than His Lordship.'

'How do you know?'

'Eric's seen them go up to the folly,' Kitty said. 'And heard them in there.' She smiled fondly. 'Poor Eric. I keep telling him he should stop reading his detective novels and try a few romances. Then he wouldn't be embarrassed by what goes on.'

'What, Miss Elizabeth and Mr

Hardcastle?' Emma asked. She'd always imagined Miss Elizabeth would marry someone titled, not a man with a profession. She wondered how far Miss Elizabeth would be able to choose for herself. Possibly no more than Emma.

★ ★ ★

Mr Hardcastle left, having stayed for more than a week. Emma was afraid to ask about the new footman in case he wasn't coming after all.

'Mr Hardcastle was pleased with the service he got from you, Emma,' the housekeeper said.

'You were right, Mrs Honey,' Emma said. 'He was no trouble at all.'

'The next one may be slightly different,' she said. 'I want you to attend the Earl of Thorncombe when he comes, but if there are any problems you must come straight to me.'

'Yes, Mrs Honey.'

What could that mean? Emma had an idea she had heard that name before.

'Where do I know the name from?' she asked William a little later.

'The father was a friend of Lord Lewin's but the old Earl died last year,' William said. 'He was a decent gentleman and His Lordship promised to keep an eye on the son, the current Earl.'

'I wonder why Mrs Honey thought he might cause problems?'

'He's nothing like his father,' William said. 'The people who have been here longest say his mother wasn't very nice either. She died a few years before the old Earl.'

'I might have heard Lily talk about him,' Emma said, trying to remember. 'She'd have been here when the whole family came.'

'No, the son never travelled with the parents,' William said. 'Cook felt sorry for him until she met him. He was here last year. No one liked him.' He paused, thoughtfully. 'Lily might have, but I'm not even certain about that.'

'Lily never had a bad word to say

about anyone,' Emma said.

'They were talking about him downstairs at Easter,' William said. 'Someone mentioned he was coming again in summer and she didn't say anything against him, but she went very quiet.'

'I was there,' Emma said, remembering. 'She walked out without saying anything and wouldn't talk to me all evening.'

'And the next week she was gone,' William said. 'You don't think it can have anything to do with him, do you?'

Emma shook her head. 'Mrs Honey told me to go to her if there was any problem. She would have said the same to Lily.' She thought for a moment. 'Unless the Earl is about to turn up with the new Countess of Thorncombe!'

They both laughed.

Lily would have laughed, too, Emma reflected when she was alone in her room. Lily was the last person to want to be a Countess or a Lady. Emma hoped wherever she was, Lily had a chance to meet her handsome valet. Lily would have listened to Emma wondering if she would ever see the tall man with the stray lock of hair again.

Then, one morning at breakfast . . .

'This is Thomas,' the butler announced. 'The new footman. Make him welcome.'

Emma felt herself blushing as the staff all started shifting along to make more space at the table. She was relieved that he ended up sitting further down on her side of the table so she was not required either to look at him or speak to him.

'Hello, Thomas,' Cook said. 'Have you come far this morning?'

He named a big house four or five miles distant. Ada served him with porridge and tea and he looked up at her with a sweet smile.

'Thank you,' he said. 'This is most welcome.'

Ada blushed and returned to her seat. She wasn't used to thanks, Emma knew. Well, none of them were.

'What did you do there?' Cook asked.

'Second footman, I'd guess.'

'That's right.'

Emma glanced along the table and noticed the high cheekbones and firm jaw of the new member of staff before turning quickly back to her breakfast.

'Is it a bigger household than this one?' someone asked.

'Not that much bigger,' Thomas replied. 'But more staff, I'd say.'

William hadn't moved and didn't join in the questioning. Emma noticed he had barely glanced at the new footman. Eventually Thomas looked over at him and caught his eye.

'I'm guessing it's you I'm to be paired with.'

William said, 'I'm the first footman, certainly. But nobody has explained to me what your role will be.' William's gaze travelled down the table and the antagonism was clear. He considered himself the superior of the new man, and was challenging the rest of them to be on his side.

Every now and then the butler, Mr Sewell, liked to address all the staff, usually mid-morning when they would try to have a short break and be issued further instructions for the day. It was the housekeeper who gave the female staff their orders but Mr Sewell would make any general announcements as necessary. It didn't happen often but there was sometimes news of interest about the family.

Some of the servants seemed to know a lot about the families' lives — how the daughter in Sussex had dogs she preferred to her children, and how the son in London thought he could run his parents' lives — or, his wife did.

In the servants' hall everyone stood in a group at some distance from Mr Sewell for these announcements. Later in the week when Thomas started, Mr Sewell took it upon himself to come into the servants' hall early one day, before Emma and one or two of the others had got downstairs for their morning break. Emma stood by the open door, not wanting to interrupt by making her way further into the room.

She felt rather than heard Thomas as he found a space beside her, behind her right shoulder.

Emma held her breath as she became very conscious of the man by her side — the very manliness of him. Standing by William never felt like this. Emma shifted from one foot to the other and settled herself a little closer. He was warm — and so alive. If she turned, she thought, his arms would go around her and her heart would be pressed against his chest. She lost all awareness of her surroundings.

When Mr Sewell finished speaking she had no idea what he'd said, but thought it was not her imagination that Thomas also lingered close to her a little longer than he needed to.

3

Apart from her visits to the garden, there was often an outing to church on a Sunday. After Thomas started, he, William and Thomas went with the family in the carriage so Emma didn't have a chance to talk to them on the walk there.

She found herself instead, a couple of Sundays later, alongside Kitty who was dawdling to let Eric catch up with her while keeping an eye out for Mr Sewell and Mrs Honey to make sure the butler and housekeeper didn't spot what she was doing.

'One Sunday before you came,' Kitty told Emma, 'when Her Ladyship heard that the Queen and Prince Albert walked to church with their household, Lord and Lady Lewin came with us, walking up ahead.'

'Only once?' Emma laughed.

'Yes,' Kitty said. 'And Mrs Honey told Mr Sewell the Queen's walk was longer.'

Emma realised after church that she'd hardly spoken to William in two weeks — and hadn't spoken to Thomas at all. The two young men were always working together, or William had sent Thomas to do a job he didn't want to do and was still in a bad mood. It was so unlike William that Emma wanted to weep — or shake him.

It took her a while to realise that most of the staff had taken William's side and were looking upon Thomas as an unwanted interloper and not talking to him. It seemed unfair because the new man had been friendly to all. Once she saw what was happening Emma found it difficult to make a point and engage the footman in conversation in front of all the others. In practice, because of her station, it would be frowned upon. She realised that Ada, the kitchen maid, was feeling something similar but Ada would fear Cook's disapproval if she spoke without being spoken to.

Emma's heart, nevertheless, leapt every time she saw the new footman. Rooms became lighter when he was in them and the grey and brown walls of the basement servants' rooms seemed more colourful.

One afternoon Emma had been sent to make sure the small parlour was clean and was hurrying down the main stairs. Mrs Honey would be cross if she caught her but Emma liked the light of the main part of the house as everything was so dark downstairs. She was almost certain the family were all still at tea in the big reception room.

When she saw Thomas standing by the front door she didn't stop to think that she had never spoken to him since he'd started at the Hall.

'Thomas! What are you doing here?'

'Oh, Emma.' Thomas seemed flustered. 'I'm waiting in case a visitor rings the doorbell.'

'That's not the way it works,' she

said. 'The bell rings downstairs as well and you can run up.'

'Yes, I thought that. It's what we did at my last place. But William said that's what's done here.'

'Isn't it late for unexpected visitors?'

'Perhaps.' Thomas remained still, with his hands behind his back, as footmen are trained to do. 'But William asked me to stand here.'

He didn't look at her and seemed agitated. Emma felt sorry for the poor young man and had a desire to help him. There was a crushing feeling in her chest whenever she saw him and she wanted him to like her — more, to think she was special. Emma privately thought she'd have a word with William. Playing tricks was unkind.

'How are you settling in?' she asked, surprised at her own boldness.

He seemed to hesitate then looked Emma in the eye, the first time she'd seen the full force of those deep brown eyes since that first day. She felt the same excited fizzing inside but at the same time was ashamed for going along with the others and not being nice to the newcomer. There was no twinkle in his eyes today.

'I hate it here,' he said in a low voice. 'I wish I'd never been persuaded to come. Everyone is so unfriendly. Don't you find it so?'

At least he didn't seem to include her in the 'everyone' — although he should have done. She was as bad as the rest of them. She didn't know how to reply but he answered his own question.

'No, of course you don't. How long have you been here?'

'Since January,' she said. 'Six months now.' There was the noise of a door opening. 'I'm not supposed to be here,' she said, scuttling away.

There. She'd had her first proper conversation with Thomas and hadn't stuttered or blushed or shown herself up. But he was unhappy and it was partly her fault. She could make him feel happier at the Hall. She wasn't free to do much, but that much she could do.

'William, why did you tell Thomas to stand at the door waiting for visitors?' she challenged him before the servants' evening meal. 'You never do that and there are hardly ever any unexpected visitors in the afternoon.'

William wouldn't meet her eyes.

'His Lordship said . . . ' he began.

'If you're playing a trick on him, stop it now,' she said. 'It's not fair.'

'It's not fair on me to bring someone in to take my job,' William said.

'I don't think he wants your job.'

'He may not want it but if he does well they might give it to him,' William retorted. He walked out, just as Thomas was coming in.

William seemed to forget himself and stood back to let the other man enter. Then it was as though he remembered he wasn't being his usual polite self these days and he pushed his way out.

Emma waited until she was sure William was out of earshot. 'He's not usually so rude.'

Thomas sat down. 'How long do you think it will take before he accepts me?'

'I'll talk to him again.' Emma was certain William couldn't continue being ill-tempered for much longer. It was so against his character and she was anxious to make it allright for Thomas.

'You're . . . friends with William, aren't you?'

Emma looked at Thomas and had to stop herself from staring, she loved so much to look at him. William's lips were rather thick but Thomas's were beautifully shaped and she became flustered at the thought of those lips anywhere near her own.

'Yes, he'll listen to me eventually,' she told Thomas, remembering herself finally. 'He thinks you're after his job.'

'Of course I'm not. I was engaged because of him.' There was a note of disgust in his voice.

'I thought it was His Lordship who asked you.'

'Yes, because he thought I looked like

his existing footman. I never wanted to be a footman and now I've been chosen because I'm tall and slim like William. As if I was one of a pair of matching candlesticks and not a person at all.'

Emma was shocked, but Thomas wasn't finished yet.

'His Lordship told me we'd get paid extra if we worked well as a pair and even that's not going to happen because William does his best to catch me out when we're serving. I'm going to be the one losing the job if it carries on like this — and then I don't know what I'll do.'

Emma felt a flash of sympathy. 'If you didn't want to be a footman what did you want to do?'

'I wanted to be a gardener or work on a farm but you take what comes.' Thomas stared into the distance for a moment, then got on with polishing His Lordship's shoes.

'You need the money for your family?'

'My ma's ill,' he said, his face softening. 'She's got no one but me.'

'Have you told William what His Lordship said?' she asked him.

Thomas shook his head. 'He won't listen.'

'I'll have another try,' Emma promised.

Thomas looked at her and she thought he seemed sad. 'Yes. He might listen to you.'

It wasn't until later that Emma realised what Thomas must have meant when he asked if she and William were 'friends'. She was confident she could win William over but that would only confirm to Thomas that they were more than just friends. And that wasn't what she wanted at all.

* * *

'We're expecting another visitor at the Hall soon, Thomas,' Emma announced in a loud voice in a lull in the talk at the table during the evening meal. 'Did they get more visitors in the place you worked before?'

Thomas looked startled and so, Emma noticed, did a lot of the others, as though she'd said something wrong. She felt her cheeks flame and hoped they weren't too red. She wasn't sure whether Thomas was pleased at being addressed for once or whether it was embarrassing for him.

'There was a lot of coming and going,' he said. 'It makes it interesting.'

There was silence while Emma cast desperately around for something else to say something.

'Did they have music?' Ada asked. 'I would like to hear some music.'

Thomas smiled at her. 'The daughters of the family played piano and harp but we didn't hear that very often,' he said. 'Sometimes there was a dance — nothing grand, though.'

Emma had the impression Thomas was also looking for something to say, but he would get the message not everyone was hostile to him. She admired Ada's bravery — although Ada did sometimes speak without thinking, and often without stopping — but not usually when Cook was around. Today she opened her mouth without considering the general hostility towards Thomas.

'There used to be more entertaining here,' a chamber maid further down the table put in. 'I suppose now most of the children are married off there's less need.'

'When I was a girl I worked in a house where there was music and dancing for the servants sometimes,' Cook put in.

'Oh, I wish we could have that,' Ada said.

Emma avoided catching Thomas's eyes and when the meal was over got up quickly from the table so as not to see William. He'd eaten with his eyes down and not joined in the conversation.

Now she'd upset him. But she'd shown herself that you can have some control over your life, however minor. You can turn things around, with a little help from other kind people and desire to do something good.

Emma pondered how she would make things up to William and convince him to treat Thomas better, but before she could speak to him again something happened . . .

While the family were at dinner that same night Mr Sewell the butler came hurrying downstairs to ask her and Kitty to come into the dining room to clear up some soup that Thomas had spilled. The two girls rushed upstairs. For Mr Sewell to leave the room while the family were eating was unheard of and she had never been into the dining room while the family were there.

He opened the door to a scene Emma had only imagined. The table gleamed with plates and glasses and cutlery, all immaculately placed. His Lordship sat at the head of the table with Her Ladyship on one side and Miss Elizabeth on the other. Miss Elizabeth's low-cut cream gown exposed her shoulders and neck and Emma couldn't resist the idea that it would look better on someone less thin and bony. Miss Elizabeth's dark hair was parted in the centre and fell in ringlets about her face. Miss Elizabeth was looking around the room with a bored expression and the whole effect, Emma thought, was that she looked hard, older than her twenty-six years.

Then Emma registered that Thomas was kneeling trying ineffectively to mop up what looked like the whole tureen of soup that had overturned by the side of Her Ladyship's chair. Her Ladyship seemed to be pretending it hadn't happened and was looking in the other direction.

William was standing by, cheeks flaming and looking as miserable as she'd ever seen him. Emma wondered why, since Mr Sewell had said it had been Thomas who spilled the soup.

Emma ran to pick up the tureen, looking for somewhere to put it. Mr Sewell gestured towards William and she passed it to him carefully so his uniform wouldn't get stained with soup.

'Take it and refill it,' Mr Sewell told William.

'Wait, Sewell,' Her Ladyship said, glancing at her husband. 'I don't think we need more soup.'

His Lordship nodded his agreement.

William grabbed the tureen and fled and Emma knelt beside Kitty to finish cleaning the mess.

Afterwards Kitty couldn't stop talking about all she'd seen.

'Did you see the candles, Emma?'

Emma couldn't recall the candles. She remembered the table and she remembered exactly what Miss Elizabeth looked like — but mostly she remembered Thomas and William in a state of high anxiety, humiliated in front of everyone.

She began to suspect that William had caused the incident to make Thomas look bad and immediately regretted it. He was not a bad person and he prided himself on doing his job well. He would probably be feeling guilty now.

Worse, though the family hadn't seemed angry, their reactions were unpredictable. The two footmen could both be let go — and then what would happen to Thomas's poor mother?

And how would Emma manage, now she'd had a glimpse of how much better her life could be with Thomas in it?

4

Emma thought she would be worrying all night but as always she was so tired, she was asleep moments after settling in bed. She tormented herself for a while with the thought that William had been angry at her including Thomas in the talk at the table. It was no good being in control of her life if she could mess things up so easily.

She was surprised to find Thomas deep in conversation with Ada in the kitchen when she went down the next morning. He looked as though he hadn't slept.

'What's happened?' she asked.

'William didn't come up to bed last night,' Thomas said, looking worried. 'I don't know where he can be.'

'When did you last see him?' Emma asked.

'When he took the tureen away

yesterday. He didn't come back up to serve. I was afraid Mr Sewell may have asked him to go, but his things are still in our room. If he's run away he hasn't taken anything with him.'

'I don't think William would have run away. Have you tried the stable?'

'It was the first place I looked this morning,' Thomas said. 'Would he have gone to his family?'

Emma cast her mind back to conversations she'd had with William. He didn't get on with his father, that much she remembered.

She rather thought his family had thrown him out — he certainly didn't ever go to visit them or talk about them, or send them money as many of the other servants did. He saved his wages but she never asked what for. If he was alone in the world he would need to rely on himself for everything.

'There was a servant here when I arrived called Lily, who disappeared one day without a word,' Emma said. 'I talked to William after she left. I couldn't believe she'd go without telling me and I made William promise he'd never do that. He said I'd find him in the folly.'

Might William have been desperate enough yesterday to make his way up there?

'Where is it?' Thomas asked, mystified but ready to run there to look for the partner who had been so unkind to him.

'I'll take you.' Emma turned to Ada. 'Don't tell anyone what we're doing,' she said as she opened the back door. Ada looked worried. She was too honest to tell any lies, Emma knew. 'Say you haven't seen us this morning,' she suggested, but doubtful Ada could carry it off.

She had a moment's regret that this was the way her first walk with Thomas was going to be. They should be strolling, their arms around one another's waists as they were in her dreams . . .

★ ★ ★

William was inside the building, on the floor. It must have been so cold overnight, he was curled up in a tight ball.

'William!' she cried, and he sat up, bleary eyed and confused. When he saw her — and Thomas behind her — he turned his back on them and they could see his shoulders shaking. They stood back and left him until he seemed calmer. He'd be embarrassed for them to see him crying.

It was July but still chilly very early in the morning. Emma sat beside him and put her arms around him to warm him while he struggled to compose himself. Thomas stood by looking distressed, and after a moment took off his uniform jacket and draped it around the two of them.

'Thomas . . . I'm so sorry,' William croaked.

Thomas reached down to help him up from the floor and eased him onto the stone seat.

'I was so afraid I'd lose my job, and now I think we both will.' William gave

48

a little laugh that was more like a sob.

'It may still be all right,' Thomas said. 'Nobody said anything or looked for you.'

William glanced up at him unhappily. 'If only one of us stays, it should be you.'

'I think it will be both of us.'

'Thomas,' Emma urged. 'Tell William what His Lordship told you.'

Thomas hesitated, then said, 'I was asked to come and work here because I look like you. His Lordship said to my master, 'I've a good man the image of yours. I've a mind to offer him more than you give him, and my own man too, for the sake of having a tall handsome pair as they'd make'.'

'What, they traded you like horse flesh?' Emma said. 'Didn't you have a say in it?'

'I didn't feel as though I could refuse,' Thomas said. ''My man's good too,' my master said, 'but I won't stand in his way if you make him an offer'. I thought about the extra money for my ma and wasn't going to turn it down.'

'Is that what His Lordship said?' William began thoughtfully. 'A handsome tall pair?'

'Except now he'll be saying 'a clumsy pair who throw soup about and aren't at their posts when you need them',' Thomas said.

William laughed. 'If he gives me another chance, will you?' he asked Thomas. Thomas held out his hand and William shook it heartily. 'Back to work then, all of us,' William said.

'Where were you going to go, William?' Emma asked as they left the folly.

'I hadn't got as far as thinking about that. I was working out how I could get into my room with no one seeing me and then how to get my savings to my ma without my pa seeing. She'd give it to him if he asked,' William said sadly. 'But he'd hurt her for the pleasure of hurting her, it seems, and then take it. Don't tell me it's the same in your family.'

'No, but I've seen it,' Thomas replied. 'I can't abide men who hurt women just because they have the power over them.'

'Nor me. My ma made me go for my own safety, and I only left because I knew it was for hers as well. If I thought I could protect her, I would have stayed, but me being there made it worse.' William's voice was husky as he remembered. 'My pa didn't like it that she cared for me and she couldn't hide that she did.'

Thomas glanced at William. 'It sounds as though you did the right thing,' he said, 'however sad it is.' Then he added something that chimed with Emma's feelings. 'We don't have many choices but it's important to make the right one when a chance comes along.'

Emma knew he was right. But how did you know you were making the right one?

★　★　★

Kitty and Eric caught up with Emma on the way to church on Sunday. William and Thomas were again in the carriage with the family — evidently His Lordship enjoyed showing them off enough to overlook the incident at the evening meal the other night — and the butler and housekeeper were walking in front and turning round every minute to ensure the rest of the staff were behaving themselves. They had already stopped Kitty and Eric from walking together once.

'Who is the man Mr Sewell is nodding to?' Emma asked as they approached the church.

'It's Silas, his nephew — his brother's son,' Kitty said. 'He keeps the inn here in the village, the one we've just passed.'

'Wasn't there a robbery of the inn too?' Emma remembered.

Kitty nodded. 'Worse, Eric told me, they broke everything they didn't take.'

'Why would they do that?' Emma wondered.

Mr Sewell made sure Eric and Kitty weren't together at the gate to the church but once inside, Emma slipped in beside Kitty. With a bit of shuffling she manoeuvred Eric into her seat and was rewarded by grateful glances and smiles.

Well, she would want someone to do the same for her, wouldn't she?

Next morning Cook reprimanded Emma at breakfast, after she'd arrived late again. She'd daydreamed her way through some of her early morning tasks, wondering how Thomas saw her and if she was right to think he might consider anything more. She couldn't continue her scrubbing and imagine him beside her in the church pew at the same time.

'Emma, I won't have Ada held up with you being constantly late for breakfast.' It seemed as though Cook was trying to be cross but was too busy thinking about the thousand things she had to do that day. 'It will be a slice of bread for you next time.'

Ada dolloped her out an extra large portion of porridge, one eye on Cook to make sure she wasn't looking.

'It's only the thought of Ada's porridge that gets me through my morning tasks,' Emma said, attacking it.

Thomas slipped in quietly and sat opposite Emma. He smiled sweetly up at the little kitchen maid. 'Thank you, Ada,' he said then, still smiling, turned his eyes on Emma and held her gaze.

Emma's appetite suddenly departed.

It felt as though there were a million messages in that one look. She couldn't twist her lips into a smile and couldn't break the gaze. That was all it took. That wasn't the look someone gave a friend. She was lost.

5

Later, when they were seated quietly in the servants' hall doing some mending, Emma asked Kitty, 'Do you think the Earl of Thorncombe is coming as a possible husband for Miss Elizabeth?'

She wasn't ignoring what William had told her, but had in her head the image of a dashing young man full of laughter.

'I don't know.' Kitty shook her head. 'I would have thought his lack of land and money might be an obstacle.'

'What, the Earl is poor?'

'Well, poor may not be the right word. You and I could live very nicely on his meagre income. But Mr Hardcastle has more. Eric overheard His Lordship say as much.'

'Surely they would never let someone like him marry Miss Elizabeth?' Emma said. 'Even if she wanted to.'

'She's over twenty-one,' Kitty said.

'Would you marry for money?' Emma asked.

Kitty considered. 'Yes,' she said. 'Everything's easier when you have money. Would you?'

Emma didn't need to think about it.

'I shall be lucky if anyone asks me, with or without a fortune,' she said. 'But if I had my choice I'd only marry for love. I think however little you have life will be easier if you have love.'

The two girls sat for a moment with their individual dreams, Emma wondering if she would have her choice and if not, whether she would settle for second best with someone else.

There was a pause and then Kitty changed the subject. 'Was that a letter from your family the other day?'

'It was,' Emma said. 'I'm worried about my sister. They'll need to send her out to earn money soon — my pa had an accident and can't work.'

'How old is she?' Kitty asked.

'She's fifteen.'

'More than old enough to be sent out, then.'

'Yes,' Emma agreed. 'I got my first position when I was younger than that, as maid of all work in a small household not far from where my family lived. They've had to move now because our cottage is needed for the new farmhand now that Pa can't work.'

'So you've never seen their new house?'

'No. I think it's near where we were before.'

'Why did you leave your first position?'

'After I'd been there five years the man of the house died and his wife went to live with her son, but she made sure I had somewhere to go.' Emma smiled at the memory of the good woman. 'She was a distant relative of Her Ladyship and sent me here with a recommendation.'

'You were lucky,' Kitty commented.

'I was,' Emma agreed. 'It's well overdue Agnes going out to work. If only they can find her something with a good employer.'

She worried they may have had to send Agnes up to the big house, if there was such a thing near the new cottage. With Pa injured and the only other regular money coming in being what Jimmy made when his labour was needed at the local farm, and what Ma could make by taking laundry in, her wage could make a difference. Jimmy's uncle had tried hard to get him apprenticed but Jimmy must be four-teen by now and the carpenter could be hoping for a younger boy.

'But Agnes is . . . fragile,' Emma went on. 'Her health has never been good.' She thought about how her sister had ailed through most of her childhood. 'I don't know how she'll manage. Ma takes in washing and mending when she can and Agnes helps but now they're saying Agnes's eyesight is fading so she can't sew for long.'

'When will you see them again?' Kitty asked. 'They're not local, are they?'

'I have an agreement with Her

Ladyship through my previous mistress that I can save up my days off and go home sometimes. When my wage is paid I'll ask to go for a few days.'

Emma longed to see her home and her beloved family and make sure all was well with Agnes.

Kitty was calm and easy to talk to and happy to share her own dreams. Eric was hopeful of being promoted one day and getting a cottage in the grounds. Emma thought that, despite what she'd said, Kitty would probably prefer Eric without much money to a loveless match. If only there were prospects of a house to live in for footmen as well, Emma thought.

* * *

By the time Thomas came in, Kitty had hurried to her next task and Emma was getting afraid Mrs Honey would be in soon to rush her out.

'Don't let me disturb you,' Thomas said.

'Do footmen do mending?' Emma asked, to make sure he didn't run away.

'We mend our own clothes,' Thomas said, sitting at the end of the table. He caught her eye as he sat down and she hesitated in her stitching.

Now would not be the moment to prick her finger and risk getting blood on her garment, but the idea of Thomas getting up and kissing her fingertip made it tempting.

After a moment of silence William joined them. 'The Earl is on his way,' he announced.

This caused Emma to pause.

'Oh,' she said. 'I got his room ready so long ago I thought he wasn't coming.'

'I've heard His Lordship complaining he's not as reliable as his father,' Thomas said. 'Did the old Earl ever stay here, William?'

'Yes. He was a decent man,' William said.

'Maybe the son will change now he's got the title,' Thomas suggested.

There was a pause. Emma wanted to think the best of the new Earl as well.

'Maybe,' William said, unconvinced.

★ ★ ★

Emma hoped the guest would still be at tea with the family when she took the hot water up that first day. She knocked just in case and a deep voice called to come in.

Two figures, one tall and one shorter stood by the bed holding up clothes, evidently unpacking the Earl's bag.

'Over there,' the taller one, the valet, told her officiously and she hurried across the room to put the water on the washstand. She sensed he had turned back to his task but the Earl watched her. From the corner of her eye she could see he was probably in his forties, short and portly but powerfully built. This was not what she'd expected. He was examining her as well. She wondered if her cap was straight and if her hair was escaping from under it.

Her brother Jimmy had told her she looked prettier with her hair tumbling loose to her shoulders. She'd sometimes wondered how she could contrive for Thomas to see her like that. She was certain once he saw the real Emma, he'd recognise his true love.

However, feeling the Earl of Thorncombe's eyes roving over her she knew it was important that he never saw that Emma.

She curtsied and hurried to the door, eyes averted. There was a particular masculine smell about the room, of hair oil and something else.

'You, girl,' he called as she reached the door. In contrast to his valet's deep manly voice, his was quite high pitched.

'Sir?' Emma was trembling but for a mad moment she thought he might be going to give her a tip. An extra shilling would be welcome. She lifted her eyes to his.

'What's your name?' he asked curtly, looking her up and down, his lip curling as if with distaste.

Oh, dear, there was to be no tip, just an admonishment for not being neat and tidy. 'Emma, sir.' She waited in case there was more.

'All right, Emma,' he said impatiently. 'Go now.' The Earl turned back to his task and Emma slunk out, worried now that she'd done something wrong without knowing what.

She waited in trepidation the rest of the day for Mrs Honey to call her in to tell her off, although for what she was not quite sure. Surely nothing she'd lose her place for.

She was still waiting at the servants' midday dinner the next day, when all the talk was of the Earl because he'd done the unthinkable and walked downstairs to look at them all. His valet, not present at the table when the discussion went on, had not thought it unusual when his master appeared below stairs. Then the Earl had talked to Mrs Honey in her room and his raised voice had been heard insisting he had to be given what he asked. Mrs Honey then went to speak to Mr Sewell, leading to much speculation and gossip.

Emma was relieved she hadn't been downstairs when all of this had happened, and especially that she hadn't had to witness the unsavoury Earl looking at everyone, but her relief was short-lived because Mrs Honey called her into her parlour after dinner.

'The Earl has asked for Kitty to attend him in his room in future,' she said. 'I don't know how long he will be here but I am advised I have to grant him this request.'

Emma kept her head down but lifted her eyes surreptitiously. The house-keeper looked unhappy. Should she ask what she'd done wrong?

'Yes, Mrs Honey,' was all she said.

'He's a rather exacting guest,' Mrs Honey said, dismissing her. 'And he's still in mourning, of course, so maybe we have to make allowances.'

'Yes, Mrs Honey.'

'Keep an eye on Kitty, will you, please?' Mrs Honey said with a sigh.

Emma hesitated. 'That's all. Thank you, Emma.'

Emma was anxious to be out of the house if it was at all possible, even for half a minute. The kitchen was all of a flap preparing the evening meal for the important guest. Thomas came down from upstairs with a tray of glasses, on his way through the kitchen to the scullery as Emma was sneaking out of the door while everyone was preoccupied with their own workload.

Emma thought it was William who had followed her out to the small garden, but with a start she realised it was Thomas. So alike in height and form, but one bringing the comfort of easy friendship and the other the altogether disturbing stirring of an attraction from deep inside.

'Has something happened?' he asked. 'You look as though you are determined to escape.'

It was good dreaming of Thomas at night in the few moments of wakefulness before sleep overtook her, but the result was she sometimes forgot the conversations they had were only in her head. It was all she could do not to rush into his arms. He stood a little apart from her, though, and she remembered.

She lifted her hands and dropped them in a gesture of helplessness. 'There's no escape from what I am,' she said. 'I'm someone who can be looked at and not seen or looked at and found wanting, as it pleases the looker.'

'There's a freedom to not being seen,' Thomas said. 'Now I'm with William we are ogled as if part of a circus show. Which is what His Lordship intended.' He laughed. 'Fortunately, it only lasts a second and we become invisible again.'

Emma noticed that the lock of hair no longer fell on to his forehead and wondered if he put a lotion on it to secure it in place. Had they made him less himself to create the right image for the family? She supposed it was similar to her need to keep her hair tucked under her hat despite its wish to escape.

'You're right,' Emma said. 'Maids are invisible unless there is something out of place. But I wonder what it must be like for the pretty ones when there is ogling to be done.'

'What do you mean?'

'Lily is a very pretty girl,' she explained. 'And I think the Earl may have looked at her in a way she disliked.'

Thomas now looked grim. 'I can believe that.'

'Now Kitty will be in that position, too,' she said. 'Kitty is very fetching too, don't you think?'

Emma saw that the question embarrassed Thomas and she didn't need his agreement to know she was right. She hurried on, 'He looked me up and down and decided he preferred someone to adorn his bedchamber for the minute it took to take his water in, as if the water was any less hot or wet if carried by a plain servant!'

'What are you talking about, Emma?' Thomas said. 'You're beautiful.'

She laughed. 'That's very kind!'

Emma made to go in. It was sweet of him to want to make her feel better. She remembered her own attempt to reassure William that he was handsome. She hadn't meant it except as a gesture of true friendship. She could have told him he was caring and interesting and a pleasure to be with but he hadn't wanted to hear that. For life was made up of such small kindnesses, wasn't it? They didn't have money, or many chances in life, but they could still be kind to one another.

Thomas was still standing there as she moved past him. 'You don't believe me, do you?' he said. 'I will never lie to you, Emma. You're lovely.'

On her way back to work she saw Kitty going into the housekeeper's room, looking worried as she had done, and felt a stab of anxiety. It would now become Kitty's burden. Kitty had fair hair, as Lily had, and it sat neatly under her cap; she had even features and wide blue eyes. Emma didn't like to imagine the Earl's roving eyes on that pretty face.

Thomas hadn't lied to her as much as done something to try to make her feel better. She should be grateful she wasn't like Kitty. But it was disturbing to have her own freedom bought at the cost of discomfort for someone else.

6

Some days later Emma received a letter from home. As always she wanted to rip it open and devour it immediately, but she had to wait until evening when she was alone to pore over it with the last of her candle.

At first she thought she must have the Earl of Thorncombe on her mind to imagine the name leaping out at her but, no, there it was in her mother's handwriting!

Pa goes on well, her mother wrote, *and we are managing because Jimmy has work up at the farm and is promised work there all through the summer. He is growing strong and manly from the labour and is paid by the week so we are doing well. We have managed to keep Agnes with us so far. The new Earl of Thorncombe — his father the seventh Earl died last year so this one is the eighth Earl — has taken Mitchfield House for the summer, while his own property is being renovated, I understand. There is a hope he will hire new staff. Mitchfield House is about two miles from us, Jimmy thinks, so Agnes will be able to come home to visit. The housekeeper there told our neighbour it would be light work for someone like Agnes as a scullery maid. Agnes is anxious to go as the needle-work is not bringing much in. If she is allowed a day off a week to come and see us I can keep an eye on her.*

There followed wishes that she could also see Emma regularly that brought tears to her eyes. She supposed a scullery maid would do what Ada did without the food preparation. She wouldn't call scrubbing pots light work but if there were others to help, perhaps her little sister could manage.

And even if the portly Earl went down to the kitchen sometimes surely his eyes would never stray to the lowly scullery maid, would they?

The family's chief socialising was with Eastbury Manor on the other side of the village, whose land adjoined theirs to the north. As Emma understood it, for a long time the families hoped for a liaison between Miss Elizabeth and the son of the family.

His Lordship had held a ball a couple of years before, William told her, and it looked as though the two might get together, but the son spent practically all his time with a visiting lady. Emma got the impression Miss Elizabeth was humiliated in front of everyone and relations between the two houses cooled.

Cook had let slip that she thought Miss Elizabeth was getting past the age to make a good marriage and had never received an offer.

It was generally thought downstairs that the Earl was courting Miss Elizabeth. Eric the groundsman had seen and heard them together.

'Do you think he's suitable for her?'

Emma asked William one day.

'I should think so,' William said. 'He's got land and a title, even if he hasn't got much money.'

'But he's so much older than her.'

'That doesn't seem to matter.'

Emma felt no great loyalty to Miss Elizabeth but she couldn't see her being happy with the short, stout, unpleasant older man.

'And she needs to be married,' William said.

'Whom would you like to marry, William?'

Unexpectedly, William's face softened and a distant look entered his eyes. 'It doesn't hurt to dream but if our dreams don't work out, Emma, I'll marry you.'

He strolled off before Emma could question him more. Did he know who she was dreaming of? He didn't seem to. Maybe he just realised she would have yearnings like him. Perhaps he'd set his sights on Miss Elizabeth! Emma chuckled at the thought. Down-to-earth, practical William wouldn't pitch his dreams thus, would he? And he seemed all right about her marrying the Earl, or indeed anyone. More important, if he was willing to marry Emma, even if it was said in jest, that meant Thomas may not be out of her reach.

*   *   *

As July came to an end the Earl stayed on, leaving once or twice for one or two days at a time to take care of business elsewhere. It didn't seem very polite to be treating Lewin Hall as though it was his own, coming and going as he pleased, but His Lordship seemed to accept it. Perhaps he saw it as his duty to his deceased friend. Emma saw Kitty longing for him to be away for as long as possible but Kitty never shared any unpleasantness with being around the man so Emma hoped all was well.

Without the visitor to amuse her Miss Elizabeth asked William to accompany her to the village, to assist with purchases and carry parcels.

That evening William reported that they had met some people from Eastbury Manor and he had managed to exchange a few words with the maid accompanying them, whom he knew from when he'd taken messages there. This maid, Flora, always passed the time of day with him and Emma thought he was pleased to have seen her. But Emma was also interested in the man and woman. William learned that he was the one who had previously been linked romantically to Miss Elizabeth and she his wife. Miss Elizabeth had been said to have been in a bad mood for the rest of the day.

'She needs to decide who she's setting her cap at,' was Cook's verdict.

The following week there was a more dramatic story to tell, the day after the Earl had returned . . .

Thomas was running an errand for Her Ladyship and William had been sent out by His Lordship. Miss Elizabeth and the Earl were walking in the village. Thomas was inside a shop, and William was approaching the village from the Hall.

'The Earl stopped to talk to two very rough looking fellows indeed,' William said, distaste on his face. 'Even from that distance I could see that. He left Miss Elizabeth standing there while he conducted his business with them.'

'Business?' Emma asked.

'Money changed hands,' William said.

'He gave them money?' Emma asked. 'Perhaps they'd done some work for him then.'

'No, *they* gave *him* money.'

'How strange.'

'It got stranger. A villager was walking along the side of the path towards all of us, with a basket over her arm. A woman of about forty or so, neat and tidy enough but clearly not wealthy. She lowered her eyes when she saw Miss Elizabeth and the other group and was about to walk past.' William looked beyond Emma as he sought to remember the sequence of events. 'By that time the Earl had finished his conversation and taken Miss Elizabeth's arm again and they moved on. I was in the direct line of view so I saw what they didn't. The two rogues deliberately barged into the woman with the basket and she lost her footing and fell.'

'What, they pushed her over for no reason?'

He nodded. 'Fortunately, Thomas was just coming out of the shop opposite and saw what happened. He ran over to help her. He helped dust her down and by the time I got there a minute later, he'd given her his arm and seemed to be escorting her home.'

'He's very kind,' Emma said, falling a little bit more in love at the thought of this action.

Thomas was pressed for more information when he returned late for the servants' tea, having run his errands. Some of the others had begun taking hot water to the family's rooms and preparing baths and dress for dinner. It was to be a special dinner that night, with visitors to show the Earl off to.

Cook had been in a flap for days.

Emma contrived to stay to listen to Thomas's side of the story — as did Cook, despite herself.

'Two scruffy rascals just knocked a woman down for no reason I could see. She was shaken so I helped her up and offered to see her home.'

'I saw that,' William said. 'But I didn't see where you went.'

'She directed me to a cottage on the outskirts of the village, in the forest off the beaten track.'

Cook nodded, listening rapt to the story. 'There are some cottages deep in the forest,' she said. 'Lonely places to live.'

'As we neared it and she pointed it out,' Thomas went on, 'I asked if there was anyone at home waiting for her. I only meant was there someone to look after her once she got in but she pulled away from me and told me she'd be all right the rest of the way.' He looked worried. 'I hope she didn't misunderstand.'

'Did she talk about her situation along the way?' Emma asked.

Thomas nodded. 'I explained who I was and she said she uses herbs and plants for healing. Living near the forest she had easy access, she said.' He thought for a moment. 'I'm sorry I startled her at the end. As she ran off I called to her to come to the Hall and ask for me if ever there was anything I could do.'

'That's good, Thomas — we'll help her if we can,' William agreed. 'What was her name, do you know? In case she sends a message for you.'

'Mary Ann, she said,' Thomas replied.

7

On the Sunday Emma was keen to find out where Mary Ann lived. By now the name was mixed up in Emma's mind with Lily's disappearance. Fortunately the family were not going to morning service so on the trip to church she walked with Kitty, with William and Thomas behind them. Emma dawdled until the two footmen caught them up, then fell into step beside Thomas. Kitty went ahead to catch Eric up.

After they left the Hall behind, there was a straight path going west that led eventually to the church. Emma knew that Hall land continued behind the rows of houses that had been built along the path and behind it on the northern side. To the south there was a row of houses and, beyond the church, the area where the market was held once a week. Behind it all was forest, patchy where the market was held closer to the town but thicker in places.

Emma imagined Mary Ann's to be one of the cottages to the south, some of which were set back further than others, and hoped Thomas would point it out to her.

'Thomas, which one of these houses does Mary Ann live in?' she asked softly.

She didn't want anyone to hear because if she decided to pay the woman a visit, it would have to be in secret. She imagined trailing behind one Sunday and hiding until the others were out of sight. Or walking far to the left of the group and ducking between two houses quickly. It was a plan that worked well in her head alone in her room but did not look so easy now she was here.

Thomas was obliging. He turned and pointed back the way they'd come, past the first house after the wooded area.

'You see that patch of forest, before the row of houses along this path?

There's a way through, though it's not very trodden.' He turned back to her again. 'You wouldn't see it if you didn't know. She has a small dwelling a way down that path.'

'Deep in the forest?' Emma asked, thinking what a lonely, dark place it must be.

'No. It's in a big clearing. But well away from the village and surrounded by trees, yes.'

Emma's idea of visiting Mary Ann alone started to retreat. 'Would you take me there one day?'

Thomas hesitated. 'Why would you want to go there?' he asked.

Emma took stock of the group around her to see how much time she might have to finish this conversation. The party was spread out over quite a wide area. Mr Sewell and Mrs Honey were far ahead and, behind her and Thomas, Kitty and Eric dawdled even more. She knew they would have to hurry to catch up in a minute. She'd seen Kitty and Eric do this before, and thought she'd leave it to them to gauge the moment when they needed to begin to run.

'Do you remember I mentioned a housemaid who worked at the Hall when I first arrived, called Lily?' she began.

'I do,' he said. 'William says you are still concerned about her.'

Emma blinked. 'You and William talk about me?'

'Of course,' Thomas said with a smile. 'He cares about you.'

Kitty and Eric passed them at a good pace.

'Better get a move on,' Kitty called.

'I've got an idea Mary Ann might know something about where Lily went,' Emma said.

Thomas nodded thoughtfully. Then without warning he smiled, took Emma's hand and ran.

Her first thought was how soft his hand was and how hers must feel to him — rough and dry from the work she did. He squeezed it for a moment before he dropped it as they caught up with the others and when she caught the twinkle in his eye she knew the roughness wasn't important. It was all part of who she was, and she thought he liked her.

Emma could still feel the warmth of Thomas's hand once she was in the pew with the other maids. And the memory of the smile and the warmth in her heart lasted even longer.

★　★　★

The next day, as Emma was scrubbing the steps leading up to the front door and looking forward to her breakfast, Emma sensed someone behind her again and stood up. She turned to see Thomas, just as he'd been standing the first time she saw him. She'd been excited to glimpse him then — just the look of him had made her heart race. Now she knew how good and kind he was he'd become even more dear to her, though that remained her secret.

Familiarity meant she could cope with the heightened senses in her body and still smile normally even though her heart was dancing. She wondered if she would ever be able to be normal around Thomas.

'Do you remember the first time we met?' he asked. 'I'd come to see about the position here and as soon as I saw you I was determined I'd take it.'

'I'll never forget that morning, Thomas.' She risked looking into his eyes. As always they drew her in so that she almost forgot herself. 'I'm glad they offered you the place.'

It was difficult to know where the conversation could go from here. He couldn't ask her to walk out with him because how would they contrive it? She determined to ask Kitty how she had reached an understanding with Eric.

Now, because Thomas didn't say anything else, she went on, 'Do you know, I was so surprised by seeing you that day I forgot to polish the knocker. I spent the rest of the day worried some visitor would complain.'

'I spent the day wondering if you already had a sweetheart,' Thomas said. 'And for the first few weeks until William saw sense I wished you hadn't. But now I'm glad you make one another happy and am glad to have you both as friends.'

He gave his special sweet smile and caught her gaze for a moment, as he had a habit of doing, then hurried away. 'I have to get on with cleaning the boots,' he said as he went. 'And you mustn't forget the brass knocker.'

Emma was shocked. Had she understood correctly what he had said? He thought she and William were courting?

She had been too surprised to correct his assumption straight away and the more she thought it round in circles the more she wondered if it was right not to have. Suppose William had not been jesting when he said he'd marry her and that was his hope all along? You couldn't always tell with William. She rather thought he had a fancy for Flora from the Manor, but William never talked of such things. Suppose it were her all along? On the other hand, Thomas had said he would like to court her if William wasn't! Shouldn't she grasp that opportunity? Even if it destroyed her friendship with William?

Emma drove herself half mad thinking it all over. Only later did she remember she'd forgotten the brass doorknocker — again.

★ ★ ★

'Thank you for making sure we got to church on time on Sunday,' Emma commented to Kitty that afternoon. 'You and Eric are good at stealing as much time as you can together.'

Kitty seemed distracted. She jumped when one of the bells rang and they watched Lady Lewin's maid hurry up to attend to her.

'Oh,' Kitty said. 'If she's in her room dressing for dinner, he'll be wanting his hot water too.'

'I thought Mrs Honey told you to take it in while he was having tea.'

'He told me not to,' Kitty said. 'I'm wrong whatever I do, but he could get me dismissed. I'm sure he wouldn't hesitate.'

'Have you told Mrs Honey that's what he said?'

'He told me not to,' Kitty said, looking unhappy.

Emma remembered how uncomfortable she'd felt in the presence of the Earl of Thorncombe and could understand Kitty doing as he asked.

'It's not that he does anything,' Kitty went on. 'Just that you get the feeling he *could* do something.' Another bell rang and Kitty jumped. 'That's him,' she said in a panic and hurried off.

There was something about the Earl of Thorncombe that had them all in his power — Lord Lewin and Mrs Honey as well as the lowly kitchen maids. For someone so inconsequential-looking he had the ability to make them all afraid.

8

Emma knew Kitty was just waiting for the Earl of Thorncombe to leave, and something did happen later that week — but not what either Emma or Kitty had imagined.

Emma sensed that something different was going on as she went about her work but assumed it was a special dinner being planned, which would mean extra work for everyone but the possibility of leftovers for the staff. She half hoped it was a ball. She'd love to hear music and try to get a glimpse of the ladies in their finery.

Gradually Emma realised that travel arrangements were being made because a hire carriage was talked about. The Earl hadn't come in his own carriage — in fact, talk was that he didn't have one — perhaps he really was hard up.

There was hardly anyone else around

when Emma realised the housekeeper and butler were deep in discussion in Mrs Honey's parlour, with the door open. It would be foolish not to stay and listen, she thought, especially once Lily's name was mentioned.

'But you didn't know about young Lily,' Mr Sewell said.

Emma wished she'd heard what had gone on before she arrived.

Mr Sewell went on, 'It seems that he always gets his own way. I don't know how.'

'Not with the arrangements for my staff, he doesn't,' Mrs Honey said.

'Lord Lewin has approved it,' Mr Sewell said.

'But not specified who we send,' Mrs Honey said. 'I'll tell them I need Kitty here.'

'No. Let the Earl know she's not the best one for the job he wants doing.' Mr Sewell coughed. 'We have his interests at heart, after all.'

Emma got ready to flee as she heard the swish of Mrs Honey's skirts as she stood up.

'That, Mr Sewell, is a very good idea,' Mrs Honey said, sounding pleased. 'We'll send Ada instead of Kitty. Emma will look after her.'

Emma only just had time to escape being seen as Mrs Honey swept out of her room.

★   ★   ★

Nothing was said for the rest of the day and for a while Emma thought she would burst with curiosity and then she thought the plans, whatever they had been, must have fallen through.

But next morning Ada was full of news.

'Emma, you'll never guess,' she burst out. 'You and me and Connie and Jean are going to the Earl's house to help with his spring cleaning.'

'To Thorncombe? But it's not spring.'

'No. Thorncombe's being renovated. He's taken another house but hasn't got all his staff. I wonder if he wants to take Miss Elizabeth there? So we're going to clean it and get it ready for them. Do you think he plans to marry Miss Elizabeth?'

'It looks like it. It's odd, though. I wonder why he doesn't just hire staff when he gets there?'

'He's not going until later,' Ada went on hurriedly. 'Cook says he just likes to make life difficult for other people, including her, but then she said I'm a good worker and can go if I want to. Don't you want to go, Emma? We'll see some of the world.'

'I do want to go, Ada. I have reason to think the new house is near my family and I haven't seen them in so long.' Emma couldn't stop a big smile from forming. 'I do so want to go.'

It would be bittersweet saying goodbye to Thomas, so she made sure not to have a private conversation with him before they left. There was barely time for conversation and individual goodbyes anyway with all the preparations to make. William was certain he would be asked to go to London with the family and it seemed that Thomas may be left behind. Emma didn't want him to be unhappy — of course she didn't — but she hoped he would have time to miss her.

On their last night the servants' hall seemed subdued. The travellers were feeling a little anxious, Emma felt, and those to be left behind seemed to be either looking forward to a quieter time or, like Cook, worried about the extra workload.

'Cook has arranged for me to help her in the kitchen in Ada's absence,' Kitty told Emma. 'I don't know why because on the days Ada's with her family and I do it, she does nothing but grumble.'

'Ah, but Cook likes to grumble,' Emma said. 'She'd ask someone else if she truly thought you weren't good at it.'

'That's true, I suppose.'

'And look how much closer you'll be to the back door,' Emma pointed out.

Kitty laughed. 'With Cook's eyes on

me the whole time I feel further away than ever,' she said. 'But you're right. We all have to take our opportunities as they arise.'

At the evening meal Emma caught Thomas's eye and he gave her a slow smile. Her heart began to pound as she smiled back and kept her eyes on him. The smile gradually faded from his beautiful lips but remained at the edges of his deep dark brown eyes.

That, she thought as he hurried off to serve at the family meal, would be the image she would carry with her on her journey.

★ ★ ★

Last January Emma had travelled from her home to Lewin Hall by post. The journey had seemed endless. She'd never been so far before and never travelled alone. There had been two changes. Today the coachman indicated they would only stop once for a brief while. If Mitchfield House was only a mile or two from her family, and if, as Ma had said, they hadn't moved very far, the January journey couldn't have been so long. They may even pass the cottage today and she wouldn't know. Suppose she were to see Ma on the road?

Ada had been nervous since early morning. She was very young, Emma thought. Cook had wanted them to wait until after dinner but the hire carriage was due to come at eleven o'clock. She'd sent them off with a hunk of bread each and — Emma thought — a tear in her eye.

How different from Emma's solitary trip at the beginning of the year. Today the four girls hardly stopped talking all through the journey. To start with they'd all questioned Emma about her family, and she found out that Connie and Jean hadn't seen theirs for a long time either. Ada's lived in the village beyond the other big house and she was allowed to go every couple of weeks.

'How many brothers and sisters do

you have, Emma?' Jean had asked. 'You must be looking forward to seeing them.'

Emma was more than happy to talk about them all. It took her mind off the feeling that this was like being lifted from a place of safety and cast out to fend for yourself.

In truth she knew the servants were no safer in the Hall than in any position where an employer could decide tomorrow they had no more need of them, or someone you worked with could make up a tale about you and have you dismissed.

But there was a feeling of security based on familiarity and the moment the hire carriage drove off and picked up speed it was gone. They were all four sitting outside, with the luggage inside, and Ada was worried about falling.

Early on in the journey a strange thing happened when for a brief second Emma was sure she caught a glimpse of Lily in the village. She was wearing a woollen dress and had a big shawl around her, with her fair hair streaming outside it rather than pulled back in a bun, and her lovely face plumper and rosier. Emma blinked and Lily had disappeared — or, she reasoned, the girl who looked like Lily had disappeared. Lily would not be in the village yet not get a message to her.

Then, after they left the village a kind of exhilaration took hold of her. Yes, there were risks out in the wider world, but what possibilities too!

She turned her mind to the questions, happy to talk about her family. 'There's Agnes, she's fifteen and she's the clever one of the family, like our pa. Then Jimmy, he's fourteen like you, Ada. He's clever as well. They've been trying to get him apprenticed to a carpenter.' Funny to think that little Jimmy could marry now, if their parents gave permission. As she talked about the younger boys she longed more than ever to see them all. 'I can't believe I'll see them soon. I'm sorry you can't all go home as well. Jean, you've got a big family too, haven't you?'

By the time they'd all talked about their families they were well away from the Hall and Ada had stopped being afraid she'd fall off of the carriage.

'How long will we be away?' Ada asked.

'Three or four weeks, Mrs Honey thought,' Emma said. She had a letter for the housekeeper in the house they were going to, telling her to make sure Emma got away once a week if she could get there and back in a day, but at least twice if it involved an overnight stay.

'Mrs Honey said the house the Earl has taken wouldn't be less grand than the Hall, and think how long that takes us all,' Jean commented. 'He likes to think he's better than His Lordship.'

'Mrs Honey never said that!' Ada exclaimed, horrified.

'No,' Jean laughed. 'I did. And I'm right, aren't I?'

Emma began to hope they'd be away more than four weeks. It was fun being with the other girls. She knew spring cleaning was hard work but if they were allowed to talk and laugh it would be like a holiday.

After a while Emma began to drowse despite the discomfort and the unease of thinking someone could fall. Ada slept too, her head falling against Emma's shoulder and Emma felt a rush of affection for the little kitchen maid. They'd all been up early getting some of their daily tasks done at the Hall before setting off for more work. She wondered how the others would manage without them.

There would be less to do once the family departed for London. The Earl was to leave the next day and Emma hoped that event took place smoothly for Kitty's sake. Then the family would leave for the house of their married son in London. It would be a very small number left at the Hall.

The only reason Emma felt sorry she wasn't left there was that she wouldn't be seeing Thomas.

She thought she might have said the name aloud when the word 'Thomas' began to sound in her ears but it was Connie and Jean.

Connie was asking, 'When will Thomas arrive?'

Emma started awake. 'Thomas is coming to where we're going? To Mitchfield House?'

Jean snorted. 'I know, ridiculous, isn't it? To help with the heavy work.' She sniffed in disdain. 'As if footmen ever do heavy work. They're only fit for laying the table and spooning out vegetables. The heaviest thing those two ever carry is Her Ladyship's card round to someone else's house.'

Connie laughed. 'The real question is how the Earl managed to get all of us off His Lordship.'

'That is a good question,' Jean said. 'It can't just be because he wants him to take his daughter off his hands.'

'Jean!' Connie said.

'It's true. If Miss Elizabeth doesn't marry this one she'll have had her last chance. Mark my words, if it was the Earl's decision he'd have asked by now. He's getting as much out of them as he can in return.'

'I'd have thought he'd give them things, not the other way round. He's no beauty,' Connie said.

'He makes my flesh crawl!' Jean shuddered and Emma knew exactly how she felt.

'So it was his idea to send Thomas as well?' Emma asked.

'It was all his idea,' Jean told her. 'He was complaining about how long the renovations of Thorncombe were going to take and that his agent had taken a house for him to live in but it was miles from anywhere and there were no staff and it was in almost as bad a state of repair as Thorncombe. He said he wished he had as good servants as His Lordship and before he knew it, His Lordship had been persuaded to offer us all to go and help.'

'How do you know all this?' Emma asked.

'Mr Sewell doesn't always speak in a quiet voice when he's telling family secrets,' Jean said.

Emma couldn't criticise — she learned a lot from overhearing as well.

'Lady Lewin's maid said they're so pleased he found somewhere out of the district they'd do anything to speed him on his way,' Connie added.

'Cook says it's because Lord Lewin promised the old Earl he'd look after his son,' Ada said.

Jean nodded. 'There is that. And of course because we have a habit with Eastbury Manor of helping one another it doesn't seem so unusual.'

'You and Connie went for the ball that time, didn't you?' Ada said. 'I wish I could have gone.'

'But why Thomas as well? There won't be any visitors,' Emma said.

'Unless we're going to be allowed to make calls in the carriage.' Jean laughed. 'Imagine turning up at your family in a carriage with a footman in all his finery, Emma!'

Emma smiled. Her family would hate it, thinking she'd risen too far above them.

'I think the Earl's jealous of His Lordship,' Connie said. 'He wants to get one of his footmen away from him so he's not so impressive when he's out in society.'

'But His Lordship is above the Earl in society, with or without footmen,' Emma said.

'Yes, but appearances are everything,' Jean said. 'We may be nothing and you think they don't see us but us lot arriving will make him seem very important in the district.'

'And Thomas arriving next week will be another reason for the neighbours to gossip and speculate,' Connie said.

'Even though he'll be more for show than actually getting any real work done,' Jean added.

Emma closed her eyes again, not wanting to get involved in any more gossip for the moment — although if she'd realised how much information these two girls possessed, she might have tackled them before! For now, she wanted to nurse the thought to herself. Away from the restrictions they knew, the possibility of seeing her family, and now the prospect of Thomas arriving soon.

9

Despite what they'd expected, Mitchfield House was somewhat smaller than the Hall, but still grand enough, with a gatehouse and a long drive up to an impressive building.

The man in the gatehouse questioned them closely about their reasons for being there and Emma was afraid they were about to be turned away. He appeared not to have been told of their impending arrival and the conversation put the four maids all of a fluster. In the end, grumbling that no one ever told him anything, he waved them through. 'If she doesn't answer the door, go round the back. It's always open,' the man told them.

'It's a good thing we're not thieves,' Jean said as they drove on.

'Do you think that means we're to knock at the front?' Emma said.

They agreed, a little doubtfully, to try. After watching the hire carriage turn around and head back towards the gatehouse they stood for a moment before the front steps, with their bags around them. Then Emma marched up to the front door and knocked loudly. The brass knocker hadn't been polished for many a long month. She worried for the state of the rest of the house.

No one answered, which didn't surprise them, so they tried at the back and just as the man had said the door was open. They tried the bell just in case but nobody came.

As they stepped inside Emma saw that everything looked unkempt. As in the Hall, through the door there was a passageway with bells marked for the different rooms upstairs and opposite them doors to the kitchen and servants' hall, which both stood open.

Emma took charge again and stepped into the kitchen. 'Hello?' she called. 'Is anyone in?'

The kitchen was a mess of dirty

plates and glasses as if no one had cleared up after a party.

Emma called again and walked down the rest of the passage and through the open door of what seemed to be the housekeeper's parlour. In there, a middle-aged woman lay back in her chair, fast asleep, her mouth open and snoring loudly.

Behind her, Ada giggled and the woman stirred, shifted and resumed her sleep.

'Do you remember what the house-keeper's name is?' Emma whispered.

'Moss,' Jean whispered back.

'Mrs Moss,' Emma called. 'We've come from Lewin Hall to help with the spring clean.'

It took three attempts, each time in a louder voice, to rouse the woman before she sat up with a start. Once she was sure she had Mrs Moss's attention Emma explained again who they were. She had never seen anyone as drunk as this.

'Ah, you're here,' Mrs Moss said. She

stood up with difficulty. 'I'm off then.'

Emma moved aside as Mrs Moss left the little room, expecting her to go upstairs to sleep off the effects of whatever it was she'd been drinking.

Instead, she staggered out of the kitchen door, hesitated for a moment, and then wandered back in. She took a bottle of a dark red liquid off the table. 'I'll take this to toast our dear Queen — she's had her third child, you know, just a week ago. Or is it her fourth? Another boy, anyway. Bertie, she's calling it. Or is that the first boy? I can't remember . . . ' She wandered out, still muttering to herself and clutching the bottle.

The four girls simply stood and watched, unsure what to do.

Eventually Emma ran out after her and around the side of the house. Mrs Moss wove her way down the front path towards the gate and stopped to speak to the man in the gatehouse. They all watched as the two walked out of the gate and then they lost sight of them.

'I wonder if they're coming back,' Emma said.

* * *

It was difficult to believe they'd been left on their own but a look around the whole house made it clear they had. They returned to the kitchen. The rest of the house, fortunately, was not so dirty as this room but the skirting boards had not been tackled for a while and the ceilings would have to be reached and cleaned. At least the ceilings were lower than those of the Hall. Emma wondered if the Earl had known this when he took Mitchfield House. Nevertheless, it was grand enough and would take weeks to clean.

If they stayed. It was never intended they'd be left to do the job alone.

Jean was uncharacteristically quiet but was the first to ask, 'What shall we do?'

Emma realised they were all looking at her. She glanced around the kitchen.

'Well, we can't leave straight away because we would have to go and enquire about transport,' she said, organising her thoughts as she spoke. 'So we need to stay at least tonight. And we need to eat.'

She walked across to what she assumed was the larder and the others followed her to look inside. Emma hadn't expected the housekeeper to have been busy making jams and chutneys before they arrived, but compared to the full and ordered larder at Lewin Hall it was a sorry affair. A few apples, some flour and grains, a piece of cheese and a number of potatoes. There was some bread, something that could have been jam and at the back, various provisions Emma couldn't identify . . . but she'd seen enough.

'What do you all think?' she asked, not wanting to be the one making the decisions. 'I say we clean a bit of the kitchen now and have some dinner or tea or whatever it is at this time. Then prepare our own rooms first. Tomorrow we can walk into the village and buy some provisions and then get to work.'

Emma held her breath as no one said anything. She couldn't force them but she wanted to stay.

'Or we could just see about getting a carriage back,' she added.

There was a short silence then Jean said, 'I don't want to go back yet.' They all agreed.

Ada started clearing the kitchen table, ready to scrub the pots, as she spent her life doing, and after a moment's thought the others began to help. Jean looked out cleaning materials and Connie went to look for bedlinen.

Emma took a deep breath. It appeared as though she'd made a popular decision.

★　★　★

Much later, when the kitchen was scrubbed and they all had clean bedchambers to retire to — plus one

111

for Thomas, at some distance from the girls' chambers as was the case at the Hall, should he turn up — Emma made another decision.

'Shall we write to Mrs Honey to tell her what's happened?' she said. 'We can find out how to send a letter in the village tomorrow.'

'We'll need to stock up on provisions too,' Jean said. 'Do you think it would be all right if we looked in the housekeeper's room to see if there's any money? We can pay back the postage money if they say we have to but if there had been someone here they would have fed us.'

'Yes,' Emma agreed. She'd been thinking about money too. 'You go and look. Ada and Connie, are you happy to boil us some potatoes and see if the cheese and apples are all right for our supper? And I'll write the letter.'

The others agreed and began their allotted tasks.

Emma wrote to her family as well to tell them where she was. Maybe they would be within walking distance and she'd see them soon.

Jean reported back that she'd tidied the housekeeper's room and found a few coins scattered here and there.

'I haven't looked properly,' she said, showing Emma a bound book, 'but it doesn't look as though the accounts have been kept for weeks.'

Emma glanced at the last page and agreed. 'I believe you're right.'

'Emma,' Jean said. 'Start a new page and write down how much we found. Then we'll keep a note of every penny we spend. This won't last us long, but there may be accounts with some local businesses.'

'Is that how it works?' Emma asked.

'I don't know, but we can find out,' Jean said. 'I don't know what we'll do otherwise.'

'I've been thinking as well,' Emma went on. 'Mrs Honey made sure I got my wages to give my family. If we need to, we can use some of that. I'm sure Mrs Honey will get it back for me.'

Jean looked at her with respect. 'That's very good of you, Emma. Just write down every single penny and we'll make sure you get it back.'

Emma wondered at Jean's insistence that she be the one to enter the items in the book, but as she got to know her better, she didn't believe it was a ploy so Emma would get the blame if anything went wrong.

Once supper was over and Ada had worked out something they could have for breakfast, they all went up to their beds.

'There's no one here to tell us what to do and we work well together,' Emma said. 'We'll be able to get this spring cleaning done, I'm sure. Let's sleep as long as we want to in the morning.'

She hoped the others would agree. She had a positive feeling about the future but sleep was something Emma had been short of for so long, right now all she wanted was to catch up. Sleeping until eight would be an undreamed-of luxury.

'Suppose there are staff who come up from the village every day?' Connie asked dubiously.

'If there are, they don't do a very good job,' Jean retorted. 'They'll have to take us as they find us. I'm so used to waking early I don't know if I *can* sleep longer,' she went on. 'But it won't be any hardship for any of us to turn over and close our eyes again. Sleep well, girls!'

★ ★ ★

They didn't sleep until eight, although they managed to stay in bed beyond their usual rising time. Ada was first up and Emma had an idea it was because she was excited about being in charge in the kitchen.

They lingered over breakfast, delighted at be able to eat without being hurried to the next task.

'Do we all need to go to the village?' Connie asked. 'Should two of us stay and get started?'

115

'I think we should all go,' Emma said. 'There's going to be a great deal to sort out — things we don't know how to do.'

'Yes,' Jean agreed. 'If we all find out how to do it, any one of us can go alone next time. Anyway, don't you want to see the village, Connie?'

'I do,' Connie said. 'But we'll be very late starting if we all go.'

'We'll soon make up for it,' Emma said. 'Make the most of not having anyone watching you.'

Once outside the gate they weren't sure which way to turn. They called to a passing man with a cart laden with straw to ask the way to the village.

'Village, what village?' he asked, slowing but not stopping.

'The nearest place where there's a market,' Emma said. 'Even if it's not today.'

His response did not give her the confidence to hope for a post office and she began to think that as an alternative, she would ask maybe for a farm that would sell them some produce.

'Ah, Lexford.' The driver nodded. 'We call it a town, not a village.' He pointed back the way he'd come. 'That way.'

'Is it far?' Jean asked.

'Not far,' he answered. 'Young lasses like you can skip there in five minutes.'

It was as he said, and once they got there it was so much better than they'd hoped for, with all the provisions they needed and more.

'Are you from Mitchfield House?' the cheerful woman who sold them butter and cheese asked. 'Is it going to be occupied at last?'

'Not for a while yet,' Emma said. 'We're getting it ready for the Earl of Thorncombe.'

'Tell him I've a lad will deliver once he's there.'

Further along the baker said, 'I've not seen you before. Is there finally a family in the big house?'

'How long has it been since it's been occupied?' Jean asked, once they'd explained why they were there.

'Many months,' he said thoughtfully. 'I've a lass with a mind to get a place there. Are there are any going? She'd be a good maid of all work.'

'We don't know anything of the Earl's plans but if we find out, we can let you know,' Emma offered. 'Are you here most days?'

The baker nodded. 'Rain or shine,' he said. 'We'd deliver, once he's settled.'

They managed to post their letters and then explored to the end of the long, busy main street.

'Can we go as far as the church?' Ada said.

It was slightly outside the main bustle of the town and set back from the road, with the churchyard behind and well kept grass all round. They decided to put off a wander around the graves for another time and began to head back to the big house.

'This town lacks a tea shop,' Jean said with a laugh. 'But there's everything else we need.'

'I wonder if we could have asked them to deliver to us,' Emma said thoughtfully as they passed the stalls where they'd bought their produce.

'They might not want to do it for the small amounts we'll need,' Jean said. 'Besides, Emma, don't you want an excuse to come down here every couple of days?'

Emma laughed with delight. 'Oh, I do, Jean!'

There was work to do but Emma didn't realise how exhilarating the feeling of being free to come and go as you chose would be. And her family only two miles away. This and the knowledge that Thomas would be arriving soon must be what pure happiness felt like.

10

It was hard work, as they knew it would be. There wasn't much in the way of ornaments and small items to pack away but what furniture there was had to be covered up, carpets had to be lifted to take outside and beat, and the heavy curtains had to be taken down.

Ladders had to be found so they could reach the ceilings and the tops of the walls. There were the walls to wash and the skirting boards to be scrubbed.

By mutual consent Ada had taken command of the kitchen and in between preparing simple meals, she scrubbed the copper pots until they shone. There were a lot of them, ranged on high shelves that went around three sides of the room, but she took pride in comparing the ones she'd done with the many yet to do.

Upstairs they took pleasure in shouting to one another from room to room, something unheard of at the Hall. 'My back's aching — how long until dinner?' Or in the afternoon, 'Is it time for a break yet? Do you think Ada will make us tea?'

They took the smaller parlours first. The size of the ballroom was daunting, but they were drawn to the grandeur of the place. Lewin Hall had nothing so grand as this. Perhaps it was what attracted the Earl — he could display his importance in the district by throwing a ball to show this room off. Emma wondered if there was anyone important in the district he would want to impress.

Connie wandered into the big room one afternoon and Emma followed her.

'I'm only looking to see how much work it will be,' Connie said.

'No, you're not. You're imagining being asked to dance by a handsome Lord.'

Connie looked at her and they both

laughed, and Emma realised she had never seen Connie laugh at the Hall.

'Why, sir,' Connie said, affecting a simper. 'Are you asking me to stand up with you?'

'I am, fair maid.' Emma stretched out a hand and Connie curtsied and took it.

They strutted into the middle of the floor, and then noticed Jean standing at the door. Jean chuckled and they heard her go to the green door and shout to Ada. Emma, Jean and Connie had joined hands and were walking as gracefully as they could manage round in a circle when Ada came up to see why they needed her. When she made a fourth in the group Connie and Emma parted hands to let her into the centre of the circle and, having circled her once, the circle became two lines of two. Ada and Jean approached one another and joined hands, then backed away. They circled, joined hands, changed positions and changed partners, until Jean made a wrong move and stepped on Emma's feet and they

122

stopped, laughing with delight.

'Sorry, I must have had a different tune in my head to yours!' Jean said.

'It's going to be hard to clean in here,' Emma said. 'We'll want to keep stopping to dance!'

'Or we'll imagine ourselves dressed in elegant gowns,' Ada said, going towards the stairs.

'What, don't you like my ball gown?' Connie said, pulling her black skirts out, and they got back to work, laughing.

★ ★ ★

As they were having breakfast the next day the back door clanged and Mrs Moss came slowly in.

'Ah good, you've made a start,' she said.

She sat down heavily at the table and looked around as if expecting breakfast.

Ada glanced at Emma, who nodded, and Ada fetched a plate for the remains of the porridge.

'We weren't expecting you,' she said to the woman, 'or I would have made more.'

Mrs Moss looked at the plate and then dug in.

'Where are the other servants, Mrs Moss?' Emma asked politely.

The housekeeper looked up. 'Other servants?' Then she went back to her food.

'And money,' Jean said. 'We need housekeeping money.'

'Yes,' Mrs Moss said vaguely. 'That's why I came.' She scraped the last of the oats from her plate, pulled out a pouch of money, put it on the table with a thump, then stood up.

'Are you coming back?' Emma asked as Mrs Moss made her way to the door once more. 'Where can we find you if we need you?'

Mrs Moss turned at the door. 'Of course I'm coming back. He said I'm to keep an eye on you.'

Then she left.

There was a long silence at the table.

'That means we can stay, then,' Emma said. 'I'll write again to Mrs Honey.'

'I'll run to post it,' Jean said.

They had permission to stay!

★   ★   ★

Later Ada told them, 'I've had a look out in the grounds — there's not much proper garden left but there's a little area of lawn with a table and chairs. If you like we could have tea out there. I've made scones, but they're heavier than Cook's. I've never done it on my own before.'

The scones were indeed quite heavy, but eating them in the fresh air was a joy.

'I wonder how they're getting on in London,' Emma said. 'I feel sorry they haven't got this.'

They were silent for a moment, each, Emma thought, dreaming their own dreams. She wasn't sure whether any of the others were dreaming of the jobs they could get in London, where there was said to be more opportunity.

Emma didn't really want to live in town. She could be a housekeeper one day, though, somewhere else — she was proving she had the skills. That would be a satisfying job. Or she could run her own household, with her own husband and children. Yes, that would be even more satisfying.

They sat on for a while once they'd finished eating and Emma sighed with contentment. She had a fear something would happen to spoil this time — the Earl would arrive, or a new housekeeper would be appointed — but for now she was determined to enjoy it.

Her arms ached, her hands were red and sore and her eyes smarted but for the first time in her life she was in charge of how her days were organised. Even within the confines of a heavy task to be completed, that was a good feeling.

★ ★ ★

Later in the afternoon Connie came down, rather agitated, to the scullery to find Emma.

'There's a carriage coming down the driveway — what do you call those small ones for two people? Who can it be?'

Before Emma had time to think, much less rush upstairs to try to see the visitors before they got to the door, there was a ring at the front door.

Emma adjusted her cap and felt to see if her hair was neat, or at least not entirely escaping, and went upstairs, followed by Connie and Ada. Jean was already coming down from the floor she'd been working on.

Emma took a deep breath and opened the door. If it was anyone important the sight of an untidy maid opening the door, with three others gathered behind her, was not going to impress.

A man and woman stood there, aged in their fifties, Emma guessed, both tall and thin, he dressed in a frock coat and top hat and she in a brown silk dress

127

with puffed sleeves and abundant skirts. Her face, small and pinched, peered out of a wide bonnet that was tied in a bow under her chin.

After the visitors and the occupants stood for a few seconds taking one another in, Emma was taken by surprise by the woman brushing her aside as she walked purposefully into the entrance hall. Emma still held the door and found herself between the couple.

'Tell the Earl his — ' she coughed, 'cousins are here,' the woman said in an imperious voice.

Emma curtsied to show respect. 'Beg pardon, Ma'am,' she said. 'The Earl is not here.'

'We will wait in the parlour.' She paused and looked around the lobby, then added, 'Show us to the parlour.'

'No,' Emma said, in the same respectful tone. 'I mean the Earl is not living here yet.'

'Then send for his agent or whoever is here,' the woman said. 'Mr . . . ' She looked at her husband, if that was who he was, still on the doorstep. 'What was his name?'

'There is no one from the Earl's household here,' Emma said. She'd felt uncomfortable with the woman inside and the man outside and now noticed that Jean had come up behind her. So Jean didn't like the look of these two either.

'Who is here?' the woman asked.

Emma wanted to giggle with nerves. 'Just us.'

'You?' the visitor said, disdain clear in her voice. 'And who are you?'

'We work for Lord Lewin.'

The woman swept past Emma and rejoined her husband — or he could have been her brother if they were both cousins of the Earl — at the door.

'Lord and Lady Lewin are here?' she asked.

'Not yet,' Emma said. If just the name got her to leave, it wouldn't be a bad thing to let them think His Lordship might arrive at any moment.

She noticed then that the man held a

number of brown envelopes in his hands containing what could have been documents. He lifted them and glanced questioningly at his wife, or his sister, who turned to look at Emma and Jean. 'Should we ask them to . . . ?' he said softly.

'Not if Lord Lewin is involved,' she replied. 'Tell the Earl of Thorncombe his, er, cousins came with . . . what he wanted.'

'Yes, ma'am,' Emma said.

She stood at the door and watched the pair leave. She didn't close the door until they were through the gates and well away. Then she turned to the others uncertainly.

'Did you ever see such an ugy hat?' Jean asked.

That was Emma's signal to dissolve into the laughter she'd been holding in, although she wasn't sure if the meeting had been funny or nerve-wracking. It crossed her mind that it could have been menacing.

11

The next morning as they were working Ada came to the top of the stairs leading up from the basement and called, 'Emma, there's a lad at the back door to see you.'

They were well stocked up on provisions, Emma was sure. 'Tell him we're all right for everything.'

'Everything?' said a deep voice she recognised and yet did not recognise.

'Jimmy!' She put down her cloths and flew into her brother's arms. 'You're so tall,' she said, looking at him and then hugging him again. 'And your voice is so deep.'

Jimmy was thrilled to be invited to tea and hot scones — a resounding success this time, everyone agreed — in the garden, something he had never experienced.

'Why aren't you at work?' Emma fretted.

'It's Sunday, Em. Don't you go to church any more?' he replied.

'Oh. Is it? We lost track of the days.'

They explained their situation and he was disgusted. 'We've heard stories about the Earl of Thorncombe that aren't very nice,' he said. 'He's mixed up in all sorts, so they say.'

'We're glad he's not here,' Emma said. 'I met him and don't want to meet him again.'

'They're saying he hastened the death of his own father. Another story is that when the word got out that he'd taken the big house, a girl with a baby turned up here.' Jimmy blushed. 'Well, maybe I shouldn't have told you that.'

'I'm prepared to believe there's more than one like her,' Jean said. 'He has a bit of an eye. I'm hoping he's left the Hall, for Kitty's sake.'

'You too?' Emma said. 'That's what I thought.'

Jimmy looked around. 'This is nice

what you have here,' he said. 'Are they hiring any more? If you could find a uniform to fit me I could be a parlour maid.' He laughed.

Emma laughed, too. 'I have my wages for Ma,' she told him. 'You could take them for me now.'

'That's not why I came, Em.'

'Of course not,' Emma said. 'I hoped you came to invite me for the day on Sunday. I didn't know today was Sunday.'

'Next Sunday,' Jimmy said. 'Ma will be so pleased. Keep count of the days, mind.'

Ada urged another scone on Jimmy and he smiled appreciatively. 'Don't mind if I do,' he said. He looked at Emma. 'So you have your own personal cook with you?'

'It's a good job you didn't come yesterday,' Ada said. 'They were a lot harder.'

Emma noticed that Jimmy caught Ada's eye as he smiled and a slight blush formed on Ada's healthy cheeks.

Her little brother, being playful with a young woman? He could do worse than Ada, and she could definitely do worse than him.

'Are you an apprentice?' Connie asked. 'To a carpenter, did Emma say?'

'No. Our uncle did try to get me a place but it may be too late. For now I've been working as a day labourer for a local farmer. There's been a lot of work in the fields over the summer, but as autumn comes . . . I'm hopeful I'll be able to work through the seasons because the farmer lets me handle the horses sometimes. I'm learning how to care for them and drive the cart.'

'That's good, Jimmy — I remember you always liked the horses.'

'He's good to me, the farmer.'

'And it's a good skill to have,' Emma said.

'Ma will be pleased of a few pounds, I know,' Jimmy went on. 'There's nothing locally for Agnes and we don't want her to go away. Or up here, unless it's you four running the house.'

'We could, as well,' Jean said.

'It would be nice to show her your eating place in the garden,' Jimmy said.

'Yes,' Emma agreed. 'See if you can bring her for a visit. Not to put ideas into her head about coming here to work when the owner is settled in, but just to see. Could she make the walk?'

'I think so,' Jimmy said.

'Just a minute, though,' Emma said, as Jimmy was about to leave, remembering her situation. 'I can't take a day off and leave you all to it.'

'We'll all have Sunday off,' Jean said. 'We can go to church and then for a walk, and spend the rest of the day lazing about.'

'And we can sleep a little later,' Ada suggested.

'Good,' Emma said, happy again. 'But do you even remember how to laze about?'

'No.' Jean laughed. 'But I'm sure we'll pick up the skill as the day goes on!'

Emma kissed and hugged her brother

heartily, full of gratitude for her blessings.

* * *

'I don't know why you and I haven't talked more, Emma,' Jean commented later. 'We often seem to think the same.'

'I know,' Emma agreed. 'We don't have the same chances to chat as we've made here.' She smiled warmly at Jean. 'I don't suppose you have any ideas about where Lily could be, do you?'

Jean's own smile faded. 'No, but I'm sure Mrs Honey does.'

'I thought that, too,' Emma said. 'She told me Lily was all right but said no more. Do you think her going had anything to do with the Earl?'

'I don't see how,' Jean said, thinking. 'But it was odd that she left a week after we first found out he was coming back.'

'Had she been all right with him when he was at the Hall in December?' Emma asked.

'She didn't have any problems with

him, as far as I know. She even said one day she thought he was handsome and she laughed with us when no one agreed but stuck to her view!'

'I wish I'd asked her about him,' Emma said.

'I'm sure you've racked your brain already,' Jean said, 'but can you think of anything she said before she went?'

'She stopped talking to me for about a week before she left. I mean, she talked, but not about the things we . . . well, we used to imagine our futures, you know.'

'Yes, in bed at night. Me and Connie do that.'

'I didn't take any notice until she'd gone,' Emma said. 'I thought she'd soon get back to normal.' She sighed. 'I'd started to think we'd never find out, but being here makes me feel more hopeful.'

'I know what you mean,' Jean said. 'As though we've got more control than we think we have.' Jean hesitated. 'Maybe we could go together to speak to Mrs Honey,' she suggested.

'Yes,' Emma said. 'Oh, thank you, Jean! That makes me feel we might change things after all.'

She went back to work comforted. They'd solve the mystery of where Lily went, she was sure.

*　★　★*

Next day, Emma was upstairs calculating how much more work there was to be done and comparing it to what they had achieved so far. She lingered at the window that looked out on the long front driveway because a figure was walking up it with a confident jaunty step.

She hoped it wasn't someone to spoil their time together. It would have to happen one day soon, but please, not yet . . . As the figure drew closer she remembered who else was supposed to come and it was all she could do not to run down and throw herself into his arms, the way she had with her brother!

Despite her desire to see Thomas,

part of Emma had been worrying that his arrival would ruin the atmosphere between the girls. Jean and Connie did not seem to have any respect for him at all — or not for footmen in general.

The hour laughing and talking with Jimmy reassured her a little. The talk was different because he was new to them, not because he was a man — was little Jimmy really a man? He certainly seemed like one, so tall and broad.

She wondered how Thomas would manage . . . and how they would manage with Thomas.

She watched him wend his way round to the back of the house and ran down to the downstairs door, arriving a few seconds after he did.

'Thomas!' she heard Ada exclaim. 'Welcome!'

As she reached the door she felt Ada hesitating and felt sad that her new-found drive to be hospitable would come to an end and they would not have any more amicable outdoor meals.

'Hello, Thomas,' she said, suppressing

the desire to approach him with both hands outstretched. It seemed to Emma that Thomas stood similarly uncertain.

She couldn't take her eyes off of him. Thomas outside of his livery was a different creature to the one she had had in her mind all this time. His hair was dishevelled and falling forward over his forehead, and without his footman's uniform he looked altogether more approachable.

When Connie and Jean joined them to Emma's surprise they greeted Thomas warmly.

'You'll want a drink, and something to eat after your journey,' Emma said. 'Ada, could you manage to find some cold cuts and potatoes and we'll all have an early dinner?'

Ada began to busy herself and the meal was put together quickly.

'We'll eat in here, I think,' Emma said as the others hesitated, and they nodded.

'What, have you been using the dining room upstairs?' Thomas asked, setting to and helping to lay plates out.

Jean laughed. 'No, because it would still be us running up and down stairs with everything. If you want to serve us one day we could do it!'

Thomas smiled too. 'I throw soup around, don't forget,' he said. 'It may still end up being more work for you.'

Emma was happy to see Thomas and the others joking together. Perhaps it wasn't going to be so difficult after all.

'You must be tired, Thomas, after your journey,' she said as they sat down to eat. 'Do you want to sleep a little after dinner?'

'No, I'll get straight down to work,' he said.

'Tell us all about what's been happening at the Hall since we've been gone,' Jean said.

'Well, the Earl got an urgent message and left the same day you did — for London, we think. He went in rather a hurry. We thought he would wait until the next morning. Miss Elizabeth seemed put out, Kitty said — 'Thomas stopped himself and looked around the table. 'Perhaps I shouldn't be passing on gossip.'

Jean spoke for them all. 'Do pass on gossip, Thomas — we're starved of it!'

Thomas laughed. 'There isn't much more. The family left the next day for London.'

'That's to the married son, isn't it?' Emma said. 'Did William go with them?'

'He did,' Thomas answered. 'I think he was pleased not to have been given my job.'

'And are you not pleased to be here with us?' Jean asked.

'Oh, I'm pleased with my lot, all right,' Thomas said, smiling.

'And Kitty?' Emma asked. 'Is she all right?'

'Kitty bucked up the minute the Earl was out of the door,' Thomas said. 'She took against him so much it was obvious. Is that why you ask?'

'I was worried about Kitty,' was all Emma said but she felt Thomas's eyes on her and thought he understood.

'Does Cook miss me?' Ada asked.

'She asked me to tell you to take care and not let the others put upon you,' Thomas said. 'She would never admit to missing you but she's very fond of you, Ada.'

The girl smiled.

'She'd be proud of Ada,' Emma said, proud of Ada herself. 'She'll be a good cook herself.'

'I see her more as a landlady of an inn or something like that,' Connie offered. 'Ada likes to look after people.'

'I don't pretend to have the skills you have,' Thomas said after dinner. 'But I'll put my hand to whatever you think I'd be useful doing.'

Jean looked at him appraisingly. 'You could clean some of the windows, maybe?'

He nodded straight away. 'Yes, I've done that before, for my ma, though ours are smaller than these ones.' He laughed. 'I don't imagine you can be any more critical than my ma. She uses vinegar — is that right?'

Jean's look turned to one of approval. 'I think you might turn out to be a decent housemaid.'

'I do hope so, ma'am,' he said. 'I really want this position.'

As they all laughed, that was the moment Emma knew that having Thomas there was going to be a good thing.

12

Ada told Emma the next day, 'I knew Thomas was a good person because he was polite to me on his first morning at the Hall — but I never realised he was so amusing.'

The girls had got into the habit of going down to the kitchen on their way to the scullery to get clean water or more soap — and stopping for a drink and a chat with Ada.

'Do you want to be upstairs with us, Ada?' Emma asked. 'It seems unfair that you're on your own down here.'

'Only if you think I'm not doing enough.'

'You work harder than any of us and the meals wouldn't be half so good if I took over!' Emma laughed. 'But I worry about you being left alone.'

'I'm never on my own for long,' Ada said. 'I think the smell of baking draws you all down and I'm enjoying deciding what I do and when I do it.'

'I know what you mean — we are, too. I mean, the work is there to be done but just being able to think, *my knees hurt down here on the floor, I'll do something else*, makes all the difference.'

'I'm going to miss our meals outside, though,' Ada added as Emma got up to go.

'Me too.' Emma hesitated at the door. 'I think we might be able to tell Thomas, don't you?'

'Tell Thomas what?' came a voice on the stairs and Thomas himself appeared.

*   *   *

'Why didn't you want to tell me about this place?' Thomas asked when he first saw the space, looking around in delight at the outdoor table and chairs. 'Don't tell me you thought I'd tell Mr Sewell and he'd make you go back?'

'We didn't want to take any risks,'

Emma said. 'I'm glad you like it.'

'We'll have dinner out here, then?' Ada asked.

Thomas wanted to finish the window he was cleaning when Ada called them for their dinner and Emma was late arriving too.

Thomas ate, looking around happily. 'This is good,' he kept saying. 'How could you think I would want to spoil it for you?'

'There's a housekeeper around too, Thomas,' Jean said. 'A Mrs Moss who may turn up to keep an eye on us. She can't see this.'

'Doesn't she live in the house?' Thomas sounded surprised.

'We've met her twice,' Emma said. 'We have no idea where she lives.'

Jean, Connie and Ada got up and began to clear plates. 'You two stay,' Jean said.

There was a long silence while neither of them looked away.

'Thomas . . . ' Emma began at the same time as he began to say her name.

'Emma — I don't want to do anything that would upset William.'

'Nor I,' she said. 'But I think you have misunderstood the situation. William and I are no more than friends.'

'Are you sure?' he asked, and she saw something like hope in his eyes. 'You talk of him with such affection — and he of you. I was certain there was an understanding between you.'

Emma remembered the conversation with William when he'd suggested they marry.

'Does he make it seem so?' she asked.

'No,' Thomas said. 'It's difficult to get him to talk of such things and I haven't wanted him to question me because it would lead to me telling him . . . ' He hesitated and looked away. 'Well, telling him how I feel.'

Emma's hopes began to rise. *How do you feel?* she wanted to ask.

'But just lately,' Thomas went on, 'William has been talking about a girl called Flora and I couldn't criticise him for leading you on because he'd never talked about you in that way. Have I got it all muddled?'

'I think you may have.' Emma still couldn't quite believe he might choose her, so plain and with her red raw hands against his soft ones.

Thomas leaned towards Emma and she lifted her face to his, drawn to him and unable to resist the lure of those beautiful lips. When he gently kissed her, she began to believe perhaps he might choose her. And she'd already chosen him.

★ ★ ★

'You seem extra cheerful, Emma,' Jean said later, coming upon Emma singing to herself as she worked.

'This has worked out well, hasn't it?'

'It has,' Jean agreed. 'I hear Ada singing in the kitchen too, don't you?'

'I do.' Emma laughed. 'I'm glad not to be down there sometimes with *sweet Polly Olly-ver* and her *strange fa-yan-cy* being sung so loud!'

They agreed that they enjoyed hearing Ada so happy and neither of them said any more, for fear something could still come along to spoil it.

The next morning Emma realised they were low on soda crystals for scrubbing the wooden floors — there were so many of them it had gone down more quickly than they'd expected.

'That's a nuisance,' Jean said. 'We won't be able to get on so fast today.'

'I'll run into town to see if I can find some,' Emma offered. 'Is there anything else we need?'

'Oh,' Ada said. 'I didn't notice this morning. Thomas has just gone into town for some black lead for me, for the range. I thought I'd checked the rest of the stores.'

'That's all right,' Emma said, taking her apron off. 'I'll see if I can catch him up and ask him to get the soda as well.'

'He's only been gone a minute,' Ada said.

Emma hurried to catch Thomas up, feeling the familiar happy lurch inside when she spotted him ahead of her not far from the house.

'Young man,' she called. 'Have you got permission to be out this morning?'

He turned round and his face lit up.

'No,' he said. 'The housekeeper where I work is very strict so I escaped without telling her.'

'Didn't you think she might want to come with you?' Feeling bold, Emma approached him and lifted her face for a kiss. She was relieved he seemed as keen as she was for another snatched moment of closeness. It was a public place so they couldn't linger over the kiss but they stayed close and Thomas put his arm around Emma as they moved off. They walked the length of the main thoroughfare and up to the church.

'Have we got time to walk a little further, do you think?' Thomas asked. 'I'm interested to see the dwellings on the edge of town.'

'What's the place where you live like, Thomas?'

'It's one of a row of cottages with some land that used to belong to the local landowner and were rented out. My great grandfather was a tenant farmer but gradually the land has been taken back.'

'Yes,' Emma said. 'That's been happening where my family live.'

'If it had stayed the same I would have been a farmer, but now we sons — and daughters too — have to travel far and wide to work at all sorts.'

'And your ma?' Emma asked.

'After my father left she set up as a seamstress. She's good at it and well respected too, but her health isn't good.'

Emma was shocked to hear Thomas's father had left — she'd always imagined him to be dead.

Thomas shook his head. 'You asked about the place, not the story of my family.'

'I want to know all about *you*,' Emma said. 'Go on, though.'

'Well, it's smaller than the village

near the Hall. And nothing like Lexford.' He looked around him. 'But I'm a country boy at heart. I don't think I'd thrive in a town.'

'I don't know whether I would or not,' Emma said. 'I long just to see London.' She considered some more. 'But I can imagine I'd long to be away almost as soon as I arrived.'

Thomas was thoughtful. 'You do see that I can't leave my ma without help? I can't afford to keep her *and* a family yet.'

Emma stumbled, and his strong arm righted her in an instant. Was he talking about marriage?

'I need to help my family too,' she said.

He squeezed her a little tighter. 'We'll find a way, Emma.'

'Is it too late for you to follow your dream and be a groundsman?' she asked, looking at the row of cottages past the church. 'I don't want to stand in the way of you doing work you prefer.'

'I've been thinking about that. I don't

know if it is too late. I'm twenty now and employers may think I'm too old to train. But if somebody gave me the opportunity and if I did well, there's the chance of a cottage . . . Working out of doors and coming home every evening to you would be the best thing I can imagine.'

By unspoken agreement they turned round and started back the way they'd come.

'I hope I'm not going too quickly for you,' Thomas said after a minute. They were strolling in a very leisurely way so Emma didn't understand for a minute. 'I've been thinking for long about what it would be like to be with you that I forget I haven't even asked you to walk out with me.'

She stopped and looked at him. 'I've been thinking about you as well,' she said. 'Since the day we met and that day I felt as though I already knew you. It doesn't seem quick at all.'

Thomas squeezed her hand and held on to it.

'So you will walk out with me?'
'Oh, yes,' she said happily.

* * *

On Friday night at supper they agreed they would all walk into town the next day to stock up again on provisions.

'Ada, you're looking tired,' Emma said when the two were examining the pantry. 'Why don't you go to bed and leave us to clear up?'

Ada agreed she was tired but they still lingered listening to the voices of the others as they tidied the kitchen and chatted about the next day.

'I so like talking to all of you,' Ada said happily.

'We'll never go back to the old formal ways, will we?' Emma said. 'Not in our hearts.'

'It's going to be hard going back to the Hall,' Ada said. 'I wonder if I have a rosy picture of Cook, thinking she'll teach me more so I can be a cook myself when it's more likely she'll try to keep me down because I'm useful as a skivvy.'

'You'd be useful as an assistant cook, I'd say.'

'Do you think so?' Ada asked, hopefully. 'I wondered if I was getting ideas above my station.'

'It would be a crime to keep you down,' Emma said. 'You've got more confident as well, Ada, and rightly so. If Cook doesn't give you what you need you could seek another position, as an under-cook somewhere bigger than the Hall, or as a plain cook in a small establishment.'

'I wasn't keen on travelling far from home before but now I think I could do it.' Ada paused to think. 'Though it's you that has made this a pleasure, I think, Emma, because you could have been strict like Mrs Honey and made our lives a misery but you didn't.'

'I was never meant to be in charge,' Emma said. 'I was thinking . . . it could be washday on Monday and we can mend anything that could do with mending. We need to examine the linen and tablecloths to see if any repairs are needed or if they need to be washed. That was done as part of the spring clean at the Hall, I remember.'

'It will be good to sit together mending, won't it? I do like making plans, don't you, Emma?

'Yes, I find that I do.' Plans for Sunday and for the next week, and dreams for next year and the years after that.

After Jean and Connie drifted up to bed, Thomas and Emma remained in the quiet basement.

'I stepped outside last night after you'd all gone up,' Thomas said. 'The moon is an unusual colour these nights. Will you come out to see it?'

'Gladly,' Emma said.

It was very still outside the house and the moon had by then risen high in the sky.

'I'm not often out after dark, Thomas,' Emma said. 'But I do believe the moon is not usually that yellow colour. What does it mean?'

'I'm not sure,' Thomas said. 'The farmers appreciate the brightness of the moon at this time of year so they can work longer to get the harvest in.'

He led her further from the shadow of the house and turned to face her. 'And I appreciate the brightness to see my beautiful Emma.' He kissed the top of her head. 'But I hope no one can see how tightly I plan to hold her.'

He drew her to him, his hands on her back, and she stepped closer. Then her arms went around him and she pressed him as close to her as she could, unable to think because of the intensity of her feelings. Then they pulled apart a little and in the moonlight their lips sought one another's.

'The moon will be full next week,' Thomas said. 'We could try to come out again to see it.'

'Yes,' Emma said. 'Let's do that.'

She reached up to kiss him again and he met her lips eagerly. They kissed until Emma thought her legs would give way beneath her.

* ★ ★

'What are your plans for tomorrow?' Emma asked the others the next morning when the necessary purchases were made and they were back at Mitchfield House. She was half wondering whether it was too soon to tell her family about Thomas when she visited the next day.

'I don't know,' Jean said. 'Are you coming to church with us?'

'No. Jimmy is coming for me after breakfast. I'll probably go to the afternoon service with them. I don't know what they do now.'

'It will be nice seeing their surroundings and being able to picture them going about their lives again, won't it?' Connie said.

Emma nodded, once again wondering at the insight of her new friends. It was very warming to be surrounded by people who understood her, and she them. She looked forward to many more easy conversations with them.

'You could have asked Jimmy to break-fast,' Ada said, ordering their purchases in the larder.

'Mmm,' was all Emma said. She remembered Ada liked Jimmy. And he liked her, she was sure.

'We can ask him next week,' Thomas said.

'Oh, are we going to have every Sunday off?' Emma asked.

'The Earl of Thorncombe has no idea how long it takes to spring clean a house,' Jean said. 'Nor what sort of state this place was in before we arrived. And we already have a lot of gleaming floors, walls and ceilings to show him.'

'Let's do his bedchamber next — then he'll have nothing to complain about if he turns up unexpectedly,' Connie suggested.

'Oh, please don't let that happen!' Emma exclaimed, laughing.

'If anyone it's His Lordship who needs to inspect the place,' Thomas said, 'as it seems to me it's his money paying for it.'

'Then we'll do the best guest room first,' Jean said. 'Better get on with it now.'

And they set to with their work, nobody really believing that either the Earl or His Lordship would arrive unexpectedly and all of them looking forward to a day of leisure the next day.

They worked late into the evening and as the light began to fade, Emma looked around with satisfaction. They were getting on well, there was no doubt about it. Maybe later they would need to slow down to make the job last longer. She chuckled to herself at the idea.

'What are you laughing at?' Thomas asked, seeing her.

'I'll tell you another time,' she said, glancing around and then snatching a kiss. 'I think I can hear Ada coming up to get us for supper.'

The green door between upstairs and downstairs always stood open now and Ada would sometimes come half way up the stairs and shout out to say that a meal was ready or to see if they wanted to try the baked goods she was experimenting with. In the mornings she tended to lift up her skirts and run up, and in that case her footfall on the stairs was often enough to tell them. As the day wore on she would tramp up the stairs more slowly and heavily. Even at fourteen, a full day of manual labour wore a girl out.

Her voice as she called sounded tired tonight. 'Come on, you workers,' she called. 'I want to get to bed even if you don't.'

Thomas allowed Emma to go before him to the top of the stairs.

A scream and a thump from below made them hurry. Emma stopped short half way down the stairs, blocked from going down by the still figure of the little kitchen maid lying at the bottom of the stairs.

13

Emma felt as though she were frozen. It was as if she could see her whole life play out in her head in a split second and then Mrs Honey's words remained ringing in her ears: *Emma will look after her.*

Emma had been so busy enjoying her newfound freedom — and watching Ada enjoy hers — she'd forgotten she was supposed to be caring for the girl. She thought she was making choices at last when she was actually neglecting her duty — and this was the consequence.

Then Ada groaned and lifted her head.

'Ow,' she said, trying to get up, then 'Ow,' as she realised she could not rest her weight on her leg.

'Ada, can you move to the side so that Thomas and I can come past and help you up?'

'Give me a minute,' Ada said, and her voice sounded weak.

'Where does it hurt?' Thomas asked.

Ada tried to shift herself. 'My back mainly,' she said, obviously thinking about it. 'I lost my footing and my back touched every one of the steps as I came all the way down. My wrist as well — I put my arm behind me to try to stop falling. And my foot is twisted underneath me. That hurts too.'

Thomas squeezed past Emma. 'Ada, I'm going to try to bend down behind you and lift you under the arms to get you off the stairs. Is that all right?'

'Oh, yes, please, Thomas,' the girl said. 'I feel so foolish lying here.'

'Do you want me to hold you around the waist so you don't pitch forward?' Emma said.

Thomas turned around and raised his eyebrows. Emma blushed. She hadn't been thinking how very nice it would be to put her arms around Thomas but he had clearly thought that, even at the height of this difficulty.

She batted his arm lightly.

'That's alright,' he said out loud. 'If I pitch forward Ada will break my fall, and we don't want you on top of us both!'

At least Ada laughed.

Thomas bent low and easily lifted the light weight, but the position was awkward.

'Excuse me, Ada,' he said, evidently feeling the impropriety of touching her.

'That's all right,' she said.

Eventually Thomas himself was able to stand on the floor of the passageway supporting Ada, and Emma could squeeze past them. She ran to get a chair for Ada to sink on to and they stood one either side of her to take stock.

'I'm all right,' Ada said. 'I'll go to my room and lie down. I'll be better in the morning.'

By now Jean and Connie had arrived and were told the story of the fall.

'Yes, we need to get her into bed,' Jean said. 'This happened to someone in my last place once, and laying flat helped.'

Ada stood up, gave a small cry and sank back down again.

'Shall I carry you up?' Thomas asked.

All of them stood and thought for a while and Emma knew she wasn't the only one thinking of the narrow staircases up to their attic rooms.

Even if they made up one of the main bedrooms of the house for Ada, it would be a long way up for her and for Thomas to carry her.

'There's a small couch in one of the bedrooms — one of those funny shaped ones without a proper back,' Jean said. 'Ada's not very tall and would fit on it. If we could bring it down . . . '

'I could lie on the floor,' Ada protested. 'If you could you get me to the housekeeper's room out of the way?'

By the time they managed to get the piece of furniture down, Ada had managed a sip of water but refused food and was grateful to be carried through and laid down.

Jean fetched a bowl of cold water and applied flannels to Ada's ankle and wrist while Connie ran up to Ada's room for a pillow and cover for her. She just wanted to be left alone after that and the others hoped a night's sleep would restore her.

It was very late when they finished eating and clearing up in the kitchen and made their way up to bed, all thoughts of the holiday banished.

★ ★ ★

Emma slept badly and thought perhaps everyone else had as well. She went down once in the night, only to see Jean by Ada's bedside.

'The swelling is worse,' Jean said, wringing out a cloth in cold water to put on Ada's ankle.

'Shall I take over?' Emma asked.

'No, it's all right,' Jean said. 'You have to be rested for tomorrow.'

Emma didn't argue. It looked as though Jean had experience of nursing the sick, and once more Emma thought that she didn't know enough about her companions. She'd thought there was plenty of time for conversation but now began to fear their time here would be cut short.

In the end she slept late and was last down in the morning. Thomas was mixing oatmeal. He looked up to see her questioning look and smiled. 'I've seen Ada do this enough times — you'd think I'd remember how she does it.'

They were all in their day clothes rather than their uniforms but there wasn't the holiday atmosphere there should have been.

Thomas had taken off his waistcoat and stood at the stove in his shirt sleeves, looking younger than when he sported his uniform. That stray lock of hair was falling over his forehead.

'Here, have a taste of this, Emma,' he said, offering her a spoonful of what he'd been making. 'Is it good enough to offer to Ada? It seems thinner than she makes.'

'Have you seen her this morning?' Emma asked. She tried the porridge and nodded. 'Yes, it's good.'

'Just for a second. Jean and Connie are in there and I don't think she can stand up.'

They took a bowlful of porridge and some tea into the housekeeper's room.

Ada was sitting against the back of the chaise longue, her legs stretched out in front of her. Emma noted that the strange shaped couch really was ideal for this situation.

'Look, Emma.' Ada lifted her right arm and showed them how her wrist had swollen to three times its normal size. 'My ankle's even worse.'

'Is that right, do you know, Jean? The swelling? Is that what happened to the person you talked about yesterday?' Thomas asked.

Jean looked as though she'd barely slept. 'I don't think so. And look how flushed she is.'

Emma took a spoonful of the oatmeal and held it to Ada's lips. 'Can you do this with your other hand or shall I feed you, Ada, dear?' she asked.

Ada began to cry.

'Come now,' Jean said. 'You've been so brave so far! Thomas will think it's the look of his attempt at porridge has reduced you to tears!'

The girl laughed a little through her tears. 'I will use my other hand, Emma, thank you,' she said. 'I won't be fed like a baby and I won't have you spoiling your precious time looking after me.' She took the spoon from Emma. 'But I don't know when I'll be able to get back to standing and scrubbing pots.'

She made them go and have their breakfast and reluctantly they left her valiantly trying to eat her own.

'Do we need a physician?' Emma asked.

'We don't know one here that we can trust, and the costs can be so high,' Jean said.

'Or should we get her home so that her family can look after her and make that decision if necessary?' Emma continued.

'Yes,' Thomas said. 'That's the best idea.'

'She was saying this morning that she wanted her mother,' Connie recalled. 'And only stopped saying it when she remembered how far from home she was.'

Emma had never felt so indecisive as she sat down to breakfast. Through her worry she noted that Thomas served everyone, as Ada had been in the habit of doing, and she registered how handsome he was, still in his shirt sleeves and with his hair all over the place. Handsome and good and reliable, and able to turn his hand to anything. Yet he didn't act superior.

She loved him. Even with this thought and the worry, she noticed he hadn't told her she looked well with her hair down. Why would he care for her now she'd let this happen to poor Ada who she was supposed to be looking after?

They spent breakfast discussing possibilities. Suppose they took Ada home and she was recovered the next day? They would be jeopardising this adventure for nothing. Someone else said it wouldn't be advisable for Ada to get back to work for some days, maybe weeks. If she stayed here, could they manage if they were one short and had to look after her as well?

Emma pushed this option for a while — it would alleviate her feelings of guilt if she could in some measure make it up to Ada by tending her. Then Jean expressed the fear that Ada would probably hate it and it might force her into using her ankle and wrist sooner than was advisable. Yes — better she was with her family in that case.

'I will have to write to Mrs Honey,' Emma said.

'There may not be time this morning,' Thomas said. 'Perhaps Jean could do it later.'

Jean remained silent. This would have been the moment for her to say *yes, I will do that* or for Connie to rush in and say *I'll do it*. Emma knew then her suspicion was correct. In the normal course of events a housemaid would never need to know whether another

172

maid could read and write or not — and if they weren't mentioning it, neither would she.

'No, that won't be necessary,' Emma said quickly. 'I'll find a way.'

By the time there was a sound at the back door the only thing that was clear was that they would have to get Ada home — and go now.

'Hello, is there anyone here?' called a voice.

'Oh, Jimmy,' Emma said, rushing to embrace him and bring him into the servants' hall. 'Something's happened and I don't think I can come to visit today.'

14

When Jimmy had been acquainted with the details of the catastrophe they turned again the practicalities.

'You could still go, Emma,' Thomas said. 'We'll manage here.'

The others agreed and Emma was torn between a lifting of her spirits at the thought of seeing her family and the oppression of guilt at leaving them.

'How did it happen?' Jimmy asked. 'Are the stairs worn?'

'No,' Thomas replied. 'The hem of her uniform dress was coming down and any one of us could have mended it for her and we didn't.'

So he was feeling guilty as well. Or was he being kind, and not voicing that Emma was to blame in front of her brother?

'And Ada was very tired,' Jean added. 'She'd got into the habit once again of getting up first to light the fire and sweep the floors down here.' She gestured around her. 'She took pride in keeping 'her' kitchen well and we allowed her that pride. We should have considered her health.'

'That's true,' Emma said. 'She would never go first to bed if there were pots to be cleaned.'

Connie nodded.

'There's a woman close to us who heals with herbs,' Jimmy said then, but doubtfully. 'I don't know what she charges but I could send for her. Ma has had her for Agnes and the little ones.'

'We think we're going to take Ada home,' Emma said. 'Her parents may have someone trusted they can send for if she needs it.'

Thomas nodded. 'My feeling is that she just needs time and rest,' he said. 'But if we're going to discuss the arrangements for getting her there we need to be in the other room with her.'

Emma went to seek Ada's permission

to bring Jimmy into the housekeeper's parlour to talk. She hesitated before giving it.

'Would you like me to brush your hair first?' Emma suggested. 'I'll run up for your brush.'

'I'm sorry I cannot get up to greet you,' Ada told Jimmy as he entered a few moments later.

Emma had to admit Ada looked well with her hair about her face and her cheeks pink.

'No matter,' Jimmy said. 'I'm sorry to hear of your trouble.'

It was impossible not to note the glances the two gave one another as they arranged how to get Ada home.

Jimmy didn't know where a carriage could be hired, but thought he could borrow a horse and cart from the farmer he worked for.

'It won't be as fast as a carriage,' he said. 'And we'll need to stop often to rest the horse. But Ada will be able to lie down in the back.'

'There's an inn along the way, I

noticed, about half way, I reckon,' Thomas said. 'It looked decent if there's need for an overnight stop.'

Emma was confused. 'Jimmy, are you saying you'll drive the cart? How can you have so much time off?'

'It's been a warm, dry summer and the crops are in,' Jimmy said. 'All of us joined in with the harvest, Agnes and the little ones too. The farmer is pleased but there's less work for us now.'

'Well, that would be a good solution,' Emma said. 'To be in charge of how far and fast we travel, for Ada's sake.'

'And if we were going to pay for a hire carriage we can pay the farmer instead and for a room and stabling overnight,' Connie said doubtfully.

'It's going to be expensive, isn't it?' Ada asked. 'I don't know if I can pay this back.'

'We must write it down in the book as household expenditure,' Thomas said. 'The Earl of Thorncombe must pay — he brought us here and left us alone.'

'One of us needs to go in the cart with Ada,' Jean said. She blushed. 'To help her to the privy and so on.'

'And perhaps I need to go to help Jimmy carry her to her room in the inn?' Thomas suggested. 'He'll have the stabling of the horse to consider and can't help Ada at the same time.'

Emma was grateful he didn't say he worried Jimmy couldn't carry her, though it was true.

'Will you come with me, Emma?' Ada asked.

Emma had been half afraid she would be asked to go. Not only had she been harbouring the thought that perhaps she could still see her family today but also the thought of leaving the freedom that Mitchfield House had meant for her left her with a sinking feeling of an end to something good that she wouldn't be likely to experience again in her life. But a day with Jimmy and Thomas! And she could come back and recapture something of the freedom of Mitchfield. But what decided her most of all was that it would be a chance to do something positive for the little kitchen maid she'd let down — even though they all seemed to think they'd let her down.

'Of course I will if you want me to, Ada.'

'Is it settled?' Jimmy asked. 'I'll run to beg the use of the horse and cart and tell Ma she won't see you this week.'

Emma handed him some money to offer the farmer and the preparations were made more quickly than she expected. Ada was made comfortable on a bed of straw covered with blankets, alongside the food both for them and for the horse for the journey.

★ ★ ★

They stopped often and sometimes Emma sat up front with Jimmy and caught up on all the news and sometimes she sat in the back with Ada.

Ada drowsed a lot, leaving Emma to listen to the two male voices in the front. She couldn't hear the words but they were getting on well, these two men she loved.

In the end there wasn't as much thinking and decision-making to be done as she'd feared. They reached the inn and Jimmy didn't want to ask more miles of the horse that day. They took the rooms they were offered and the food that was available. Emma paid from the money Jean had pressed on her before she left.

Thomas left the next morning and they'd had no private time together, not even snatched the touch of a hand nor a kiss goodbye. Jimmy prepared the horse while she helped Thomas settle Ada into the cart.

There was a lot of hurry and bustle in front of the inn at that time in the morning and a carriage drew close to them, pulled by a team of big horses. It startled the poor farm horse who was only accustomed to country lanes and the sensitive creature reared in alarm, shaking Jimmy off and causing him to lose the reins. Thomas leaped down from the cart and reached up between the flailing hooves to take the bridle, speaking softly to the horse.

Jimmy righted himself in a second and Thomas passed him the reins, staying for a moment longer to pat the animal's neck soothingly.

'We should be on our way,' Jimmy said.

Thomas nodded. The two men shook hands and patted one another's shoulders in a series of gestures that spoke louder than words could.

Emma tried to catch Thomas's eye but all he did was raise a hand to Ada and say, 'Be well.' Then he wished a general 'have a good trip' to all of them and after he helped get the horse in the right direction, he turned off the other way.

Emma sat beside Ada in the cart and watched him walk back in the direction they had come. She willed him to at least look back, but he didn't turn around to wave.

Next night, Emma and Jimmy slept on the floor of the parlour in Ada's family's modest dwelling.

'It's been good, Emma,' Jimmy said before they slept. 'Not Ada being hurt, of course, but these days with you, remembering you're my sister who I love.'

She stretched across and rubbed his arm.

'It has been good.'

Ada was pleased to be home, there was no question of that. Emma had had her doubts along the road that they were doing the right thing but as soon as Ada saw her mother and the whole garbled story came out and then was clarified, Emma saw it was right.

Ada cried and said she was sorry a hundred times and was then put to bed with her younger sisters who, on being told not to touch her arm or her leg, treated her like glass.

Emma felt the need to apologise too.

'I'm sorry we let this happen,' she said to Ada's parents. 'We should have looked after her better.'

'They should never have left you there alone,' Ada's mother said, angry once she understood the situation.

'No,' Emma agreed. 'We should have gone straight back to the Hall, shouldn't we?'

'It was very dutiful of you to stay and do the job you'd been asked to do,' Ada's mother said. 'I'm proud of Ada and I don't know you, Emma, but you can be proud of yourself too.'

Emma explained how very well Ada had done in the kitchen and then the talk turned to where Emma would go next — on to the Hall to explain or back with Jimmy.

Once again Emma was torn. Mrs Honey needed to know and she was within an hour or so's walk of the Hall. But if they didn't allow her to go back to Mitchfield House the adventure would be over. She could go back to Mitchfield House now and write a letter to Mrs Honey.

But it wouldn't be the same now. It was going to turn into drudgery. In the course of her work where she seemed to be acting as housekeeper at Mitchfield, Emma sometimes thought, *What would Mrs Honey do in this situation?* Mrs Honey would go to Lewin Hall to explain in person, she was sure.

'I think I should go up to the Hall,' she said. 'While I'm so close. I hope when I see Mrs Honey I'll get an idea of how I'm going to explain it all.'

'You send her to me if she doesn't understand,' Ada's mother called as she waved Emma off. 'And come back and see us soon.'

'I will,' Emma said.

The only thing she had clear in her mind was that she would visit this kind family again.

She hadn't realised how starved of time for kindness she'd been at the Hall. As she walked her heart ached a little for the friendship she'd found at Mitchfield that now seemed as though it was going to be fleeting — an episode of something approaching freedom in a lifetime of doing what she was told and going where she was told.

The problem was, once you've seen how life could be, you can't let that knowledge go.

15

In all the versions Emma rehearsed along the way she was standing in Mrs Honey's parlour and Mrs Honey was listening to her with a sympathetic expression on her face.

What she didn't expect was for Mrs Honey to have been replaced.

She knew everything would be different because the other servants would have needed to double up to fill the gaps the five of them would have left. So she wasn't too surprised when Kitty answered her ring at the basement door.

Kitty clearly didn't recognise Emma for a moment and Emma recalled she had her day dress on and her hair loose.

'Kitty — hello.'

'Emma?' Kitty said. 'What are you doing here? Where are the others?'

'Can I come in?' she said. 'I need to speak to Mrs Honey.'

Kitty opened the door wider to let Emma through, her eyes and her whole demeanour unusually dull. She avoided eye contact.

'I'll ask Mrs Turner if she will see you.' Kitty hurried towards the house-keeper's parlour.

'Mrs Turn — ?' Emma began, but Kitty was gone.

Emma glanced into the servants' hall but it was empty. Perhaps they hadn't had their morning break yet. She looked forward to seeing them all again and exchanging news. Then she made her way into the kitchen.

'Hello, Cook,' she said.

Cook glanced up from her pastry. 'Emma,' she said curtly. 'What have you done with Kitty? For all the good she is, she still needs to be at her post. And you're to call me Mrs Dickens.'

'Kitty's gone to see if — I can't remember the name she said — will see me,' Emma said. 'I wanted to talk to Mrs Honey.'

'So do we all,' Cook said, pounding

the pastry. 'You went and the world turned upside down and I don't suppose it will turn to rights now you're back. Where's Ada?'

'I'll explain later,' Emma said, thinking it only right to tell Mrs Honey first, if she could.

'Yes, well, you might have to make an appointment through Mrs Turner. There's no chatting in the kitchen now, or next door.'

Turner, that was it. At least Emma was ready with the name when Kitty indicated she could go into the housekeeper's room. Emma almost jumped when she saw the woman, as she bore a remarkable resemblance to the woman who had visited Mitchfield House with documents for the Earl. The two could almost be sisters. Then Emma realised it was probably just the tall thin figure, the pursed lips and the look of a bad taste in the mouth.

'Good morning, Mrs Turner. I'm Emma. I've been at Mitchfield House.' She hoped she hadn't been staring.

'I know who you are.' The woman seated in Mrs Honey's chair looked Emma up and down with a sneer in her expression just as the visitor to Mitchfield had. 'What I want to know is why you've presented yourself here instead of answering my letter so proper arrangements could be made. And why you're dressed like' — the disapproving eyes studied Emma again — 'that,' she added with distaste.

So there would have been a letter at Mitchfield House yesterday. What a good thing Thomas went straight back — it would have been another worry for Jean and Connie.

'I left Mitchfield House on Sunday, Mrs Turner, so didn't see your letter.' Emma focused her eyes on the desk in front of Mrs Turner, not wanting to look at her critical face. 'Ada had an accident and I've taken her home to her parents.' Into the silence that followed Emma began to babble, all of the sentences she'd rehearsed forgotten. 'There were no other staff at Mitchfield

House when we arrived, so we've been doing everything alone and — '

Mrs Turner lifted a hand to cut her off. 'I'm aware of the deficiencies in the household — both households. Is the job finished? Are you all returned?'

'No, we're about half way through,' Emma said. 'It's a big house and we've had to shop and cook for ourselves as well. If I could stay here tonight I'll go back tomorrow and we'll get the job finished in a few weeks.'

Emma was surprised at how certain she suddenly felt. She wanted to go back and finish the job for her own satisfaction, if that was all that was left. She'd let Ada down and wasn't going to let Jean and Connie down too.

'Stay here tonight?' Mrs Turner said. 'You'll get your uniform on and get back to work. Now.'

'Um . . . ' Oh, dear, she hadn't thought this through at all. 'I left my uniform at Mitchfield House,' she said, upset at how small and apologetic her voice had become. Someone should be apologetic to her — and Ada and the others — for the mess. 'And my spare one.'

'Ask Monica to find you a suitable uniform, then,' Mrs Turner said dismissively. 'We'll take the cost from your wages.'

Monica? Who was Monica? And a deduction from her hard-earned wages after all that had been asked of her?

Of all possible scenes, Emma hadn't imagined herself fighting back tears of anger and frustration within ten minutes of arriving back at the Hall.

★ ★ ★

The uniform Monica found for Emma was a little tight.

'Ah well,' the woman said, her mouth pursed like Mrs Turner's. 'You look as though you've been living a little too well and not working hard enough. We'll soon get rid of some of that fat and have it fitting.'

Monica herself was dressed in a

maid's uniform but her cap was smaller and more elaborate and so was her apron. It wasn't going to protect the black dress from the dirty work the others did, Emma thought. She was only slightly taller than Emma but decidedly plump and not in a position to criticise Emma's curves.

'Go up and brush your hair before you start work,' Monica said. 'And if you're the girl who's to share my room don't use my brush. If you haven't got yours you'll have to make do.'

Emma trudged unhappily up the back stairs. This woman in her room? Her worst surmising proved accurate when she opened the door. The few things she'd left behind had been pushed to one side and the newcomer had taken the best of the space. Working with a new supervisor and no respite even at bedtime? This was not at all what Emma expected. She wished herself with all her heart back in the friendly company and the relative freedom of Mitchfield House.

* ★ ★

At dinner time Emma was told where to sit and among the maids she knew were two new unfriendly faces. They were not introduced to her. William sat at the end of the table looking miserable and didn't catch her eye.

Monica sat at the head of the table and when in the initial silence Emma asked William how London had been, Monica rapped on the table. The two new staff members gave disapproving looks and the old staff looked away as if embarrassed. It was like being back at school where discipline was more important than learning.

'You will address the footman as Mr Smith,' Monica said. 'But you will not need to address him at all unless you wish him to pass the salt.' She looked around the table. 'I've said it before but I will repeat it for Emma's benefit. This household has been run in too lax a manner. I appreciate you've been allowed to get used to bad habits,

Emma, but there will be less chat and gossip and you will learn to know your place.'

Emma noticed that Kitty served them and then disappeared. She wondered when and where she would eat. Was this the job Ada would come back to when she was recovered? Having to call Cook Mrs Dickens and not being able to socialise with the rest of the servants after she served them? Or worse — would there be no place for Ada?

Emma looked around the table and no one met her eyes. She no longer knew who she could look to for information.

Or friendship. Even the thought of Thomas left a coldness around her heart. What she had thought would last forever she'd ruined with her carelessness of Ada and he was right to hold her to account for it. That must have been why he couldn't even bring himself to turn around and wave goodbye. Her life had become all the darker for having appeared to be so bright before.

★　★　★

After supper, Monica gave Emma her instructions for the morning and refused to talk to her when they were in their room, not answering Emma's polite 'good night'. Emma didn't even feel she could let the hot tears fall on her pillow for fear it would provoke more judgement.

At least her early morning tasks were unchanged and she left Monica still sleeping.

Kitty was already up and had lit the fire in the kitchen. Emma risked going in to talk to her.

'Kitty, what's happened?' She thought she would die if Kitty gave her a hostile response.

Instead Kitty embraced her. 'Oh, Emma, it's awful! First we heard about what happened to you and how the Earl tricked His Lordship. Then Miss Elizabeth went off with someone else and everyone said William and Miss Elizabeth's lady's maid helped them.' The words were coming out in a rush as if Kitty had bottled them up for days. 'Well, she only went out for the evening after all but the lady's maid still got dismissed.' Kitty stopped for breath. 'And William is permanently in disgrace but still here because His Lordship wants his pair of footmen.'

'What has all that got to do with us?'

'Her Ladyship thought it was because we'd all got into bad ways so Mrs Honey got sent away and Mr Sewell has given up.' She glanced nervously out of the door. 'Although to be fair to Mr Sewell he's got family problems, I heard. His nephew is in big trouble, apparently.' Kitty stopped, her expression fearful. 'But you must get back to work, Emma. That Monica is a monster.' Kitty laughed despite herself. 'Monica the monster.'

'But when can we ever talk?' Emma asked, getting ready to flee.

'Never!' Kitty said. 'The two new girls — Peggy and Sarah, they're called

— they spy on us and take information to her. Mrs Turner came with the three of them.' Her voice broke with emotion. 'I haven't been able to speak to Eric for a week.'

Emma got on with her work and did a good job, she knew she did. She'd been a critical judge of her own work for long enough to know she hadn't overlooked anything. But Mrs Turner came past and showed her a section of the floor that was perfectly clean and made her do it again, then followed her outside and stood and watched her as she polished the brass knocker.

★ ★ ★

Emma knew it would be a mistake to look forward to porridge as she completed her early morning tasks but she did nevertheless and so it was a hearty disappointment to see only bread for breakfast and weak beer instead of tea. Emma suspected the beer came out of their daily allowance so there would be less to drink at dinner and supper, and she missed having something hot.

What was worse, the smell of eggs and bacon cooking was coming from the kitchen and Cook was missing from the table. It was too early for the family's breakfast and Emma thought it must be for Mrs Turner in her parlour. Mrs Honey had never demanded better food than her staff. Perhaps she hadn't known her place either.

They were then all hurried out and up the stairs into the parlour that Emma had cleaned earlier.

'What's happening?' she asked softly.

Fortunately it was William who was making his way up behind her. 'Prayers,' he whispered back.

Emma tried to stay close to William but Monica put them all in their places with a glare here and a shove there. She had surprisingly strong arms. Emma ended up positioned between Peggy and Sarah. Everyone stood and watched the family file in, His Lordship with a severe expression and Her Ladyship an unhappy one.

Between them Miss Elizabeth looked nicer than Emma had ever seen her look. She hadn't seen much of the daughter of the family and wondered if she had a mistaken memory of a hard woman. This was a softer looking person altogether, plumper and more rounded and standing between her parents with a small smile.

Prayers were over quickly, the family left, and Mr Sewell made a garbled announcement to the effect that there were no announcements and it was back to work.

And so that day and the next passed, with Emma watching and looking for a chance to talk, her stomach in knots of despair over the situation and regret at having had to leave Mitchfield, where it had been so different.

Kitty was willing to talk but afraid for her position. She thought Mrs Turner knew about her and Eric because a new rule had been imposed that only Cook — Mrs Dickens — could take in the day's produce when he brought it to the door. Kitty knew Eric would be bewildered and think she was deliberately avoiding him. The outdoor staff had no idea about the new regime indoors. Kitty had heard nothing of those left in Mitchfield House but she knew more letters had been sent.

Kitty was shocked to hear about Ada.

'I hope she's all right but I don't know what will happen to me when she comes back. Cook hates me because I'm not Ada and I'm fearful I won't have a job soon. If Miss Elizabeth's maid could be let go without a character, what could happen to me? Emma, if Thomas comes back do be careful. It's bad enough me and Eric, but a housemaid and a footman? They'll do everything to break you up.'

Emma was disturbed by Kitty's words. *If Thomas comes back* — what would she do if he didn't? But it was a comfort to know Kitty understood. She must have realised that Sunday on the way to church, and a woman in love recognised another woman in love. She blessed Kitty that she had never questioned her about it.

She tried not to long too hard for Thomas because she didn't know what it meant that he'd walked away from her without looking back. She worried she hadn't been able to get word to him since she'd been back and he'd think the conversations at Mitchfield hadn't been real. Did he think less of her because of Ada's accident?

Emma wondered about Miss Elizabeth as she scrubbed the front steps. Who was she in love with? Surely the disagreeable Earl wasn't the reason for that secret smile?

She felt a brief pang for the lady's maid who had been dismissed — and didn't Kitty say it was without a character reference?

Emma yearned for a long, leisurely chat with William about his situation and that of Miss Elizabeth and everything else. Since Mitchfield she knew people worked better when they were happy. It was wicked not to allow it.

16

William contrived to walk upstairs behind Emma again to prayers the next day and because he was so much taller than her he could stoop and whisper in her ear. 'Servants' hall,' he said. 'After family dinner.'

She nodded and Monica looked at her suspiciously as she glared her into her place.

* * *

Emma dallied in the servants' hall later but Monica was having none of it and sent her up to bed before William was finished the serving. The next night Emma brought mending she pretended she had to do and sat quietly in a corner sewing the same stitches over and over again.

'Bed, Emma,' Monica said when it

looked as though she was preparing to go up herself.

'I just need to finish this.' Emma did not look up, not wanting Monica to see guilt in her face.

Monica was furious but couldn't prevent one of the staff from darning her stockings, and couldn't argue there was time during the day as she'd had Emma scurrying from one job to the next all day. 'Well, be quick. You were late starting this morning. That can't happen again.'

It wasn't true but she resisted the urge to protest.

'And be quiet coming to bed,' was the unpleasant woman's parting shot.

Emma was very sleepy by the time William was able to join her. She thought about the night of the full moon Thomas had talked about at Mitchfield — it had already passed and she wondered if he had looked at it and thought of her. There was an ache in her chest.

William looked melancholy too when

he finally sat down with her and they could talk.

'What's happened here?' Emma asked, after she'd told William about Mitchfield House and about Ada.

'We all went to London the day after you left — me, the family, His Lordship's valet and the lady's maids. I've been to that house before and there's a pleasant fellow there, a footman, who takes me out to plays and lectures and the like so I didn't get involved in the life of the house.' He shrugged. 'His Lordship went here and there and I went with him as usual and Her Ladyship had me running messages and carrying parcels. It all seemed normal and then this fellow told me the Earl of Thorncombe had gone abroad without telling anyone.'

'He always seems to come and go as he pleases,' Emma said. 'Why is that important?'

'Precisely, he's a free agent so I didn't take any notice until other people started talking about what he might be running from — gambling debts were a popular notion and another one was that they'd found evidence he had killed his father.' William looked at Emma. 'Did you know there was an understanding between him and Miss Elizabeth?'

'I wondered if she might hope for it,' Emma said. 'Or her parents at least.'

'She didn't seem at all concerned that he'd gone. I served her every night at dinner and she was calm and cheerful.'

'Were the parents and her brother upset?' Emma asked.

'The brother was very upset he'd taken his father's servants.' William laughed. 'He — and, more important, his wife — wouldn't let it go about Mitchfield House. They went on at Her Ladyship something awful at dinner.'

'What, in front of you all?'

William looked confused. 'We don't exist when we're up there, Emma. Even when they were talking about us they didn't realise I could hear.'

'They talked about us?'

William nodded. 'About how things had got very undisciplined and Mrs Honey didn't have it under control downstairs. 'I like Honey,' Her Ladyship says. 'You don't have to like your servants,' says the son's wife. 'And if they don't run your household properly you have to let them go'.'

'I've heard Mrs Honey say the son's wife meddles in their Lordships' affairs.' Another thing she'd overheard.

But William went on with his story. 'It's true,' he said. ' 'Honey is running my household perfectly well,' Her Ladyship says. She's game, I'll give her that, but she was no match for the two of them.'

'Go on,' Emma urged.

' 'Your servants have no sense of their own place, Mama,' the son says — snooty upstart he is. 'There's no respect for position'.' William laughed. ' 'And I can't believe Honey would allow four of her staff to be sent somewhere else to work. Four!' Her Ladyship was quiet then and His Lordship hadn't said a word because of course he was convinced by the Earl to let you all go.'

'Do you think they didn't know Thomas went as well?'

'I do think that, Emma. No one even mentioned Thomas or Mr Sewell so I expect they don't know he went.'

'So their Lordships managed to keep that from them,' Emma said. 'But they were still angry?'

'Like a nest of hornets when you poke it,' William said, shaking his head. 'I felt like sticking up for Mrs Honey myself by this stage.'

'I can imagine you did.' Emma laughed. 'That would have gone down well. So they came back and dismissed Mrs Honey?'

'It was worse, the son did it by letter and they had Mrs Turner in an instant later — along with Monica and the other two.' William put on a snooty female voice and added, 'To get things back in order before you return, Mama.'' Then he reverted to his normal voice with a sigh. 'I'm disappointed with Her Lady-ship.'

'It sounds as though the two of them would be hard to resist,' Emma said.

'Yes,' William agreed. 'And it sounded a bit as though they had it all planned in advance. 'The late Earl of Thorncombe's housekeeper came to see us, Papa,' the son says. 'She ran Thorncombe like clockwork and is looking for a new place.' So they already had someone ready to bring here.'

'Oh, so Mrs Turner was at Thorncombe,' Emma said. 'I wonder why she didn't want to stay with the current Earl.'

'Hah,' William said. 'Maybe he dismissed her because she doesn't let him get his own way.'

Emma laughed, then asked, 'Where has Mrs Honey gone?'

'No one knows. She didn't have time to make any plans. And I think words were had with Mr Sewell as well.' William shook his head, and there was a long silence.

'How long have you been back?' Emma asked.

'About a week, a bit less. I can't get used to how different it all is.'

'And Miss Elizabeth's lady's maid?'

'Oh, that was another scandal. The Earl wasn't in London but I'll tell you who was.'

He paused and Emma prompted, 'Go on.'

'You remember in the spring there was that lawyer at the Hall, staying while His Lordship sorted his land affairs out?' William said. 'He was frowned on because Miss Elizabeth took a shine to him — and he to her, apparently?'

'I know Eric saw her with him in the folly.'

'That's right,' William said. 'More than once, according to Kitty — and heard them!'

'I remember that — poor Eric was embarrassed, Kitty said. But they made a good-looking couple, didn't they, Miss Elizabeth and Mr Hardcastle?'

'I thought he was all right regardless of what His Lordship said. He turned up in London and took Miss Elizabeth here and there and her brother didn't think it was seemly. He remembered me, though, and remembered my name. The Earl insists on calling me James even though His Lordship corrects him. I think he does it on purpose to be insulting.'

'I attended to him when he was here,' Emma said. 'I liked him too and he knew my name.'

'London's different to the country, though,' William went on. 'You can go to the theatre with whoever you like. Well, the brother banned her from seeing him, as if she was under twenty-one and he was her father, and the lady's maid got the blame for them still getting together after that.'

'How can we be invisible and yet get the blame when something goes wrong?' Emma wondered. 'How would a maid be able to prevent Miss Elizabeth doing what she wanted?'

'Exactly. But she got sent back to be a housemaid again in the Sussex house, where she'd come from.'

'I didn't like her much but that's hard.'

'I reckon Miss Elizabeth would be better off with this Hardcastle fellow than the Earl,' William said. 'If the Earl was ever a prospect.'

Emma laughed. 'She'd be better off with anyone but the Earl!'

'That's true.' William laughed too. 'I just meant she laughs more when Hardcastle's around. She seemed like a different person in London.'

As they got up to go William seemed to remember something else. 'Oh, and Emma — you're lucky you came back when you did. Thomas is coming back but none of the others are.' He paused. 'They've all been dismissed.'

Emma felt as though her heart stopped beating for a moment. 'Even Ada?' she whispered and he nodded sadly.

It was difficult to celebrate the return of Thomas in the light of the loss of the other girls who she'd looked forward to spending more time with. But it was a mercy Thomas would be returning.

'Mr Sewell fought to get Thomas back?'

'No, His Lordship insisted he keep his pair of footmen,' William said. 'Thomas was saved for the same reason he got the job in the first place, because he looks like me.' He opened the door and stood aside to let Emma go first. 'That's how important we are to them — that they decide whether we come or go based on something as trivial as that.'

17

Emma hoped for a walk to church on the Sunday but evidently it was deemed the servants' spiritual needs were being met by the morning prayers. She would have liked to ask to be allowed to visit Ada but the atmosphere downstairs did not lend itself to such requests. Her instinct was that asking for a holiday would not be met graciously.

By prayers on the Monday she'd been back for nearly a week and Emma's eyes looked for William and he generally managed a smile or a wink. She grasped at the friendship, along with her snatched words with Kitty in the scullery, to sustain her through the long dreary days and the short uncomfortable nights with Monica sleeping only a few feet from her.

Then that afternoon Thomas was back.

'More darning?' Monica said in a loud disapproving voice that night. 'Emma, you really must take better care of your stockings.'

'Yes, Monica.'

Emma bit back the retort that mending them *was* taking care of them, but she daren't risk not being allowed to sit up tonight.

After a while Emma gave up on Thomas finding a way to creep down — or would want to. She put down her sewing and rested her weary head on the table.

Emma was asleep by the time he touched her gently, turned her round and helped her to a standing position, drew her close and put his arms around her. She barely had time to whisper his name before he covered her lips with his own. After a long deep kiss Thomas sat on the chair she'd been using and pulled her on to his lap.

She leaned against him, her hands reaching up to his face, his hair, down his arms. He enfolded her in those strong arms so she wasn't sure whether it was her heart beating so hard and fast or his. He kissed the top of her head where her cap had come loose and then she lifted her face to his again. Emma's insides turned over with the intensity of the kiss and she could feel Thomas trembling. Or was it her?

'Emma,' he murmured, pulling her head against his shoulder and caressing her hair. 'I'm so pleased you waited up for me. William said you would.' He shifted her to look at her face. 'It wasn't William you were waiting for, was it?'

She shook her head. 'I was afraid you may not want to see me because I made such a mess of things at Mitchfield,' she said. 'But I did think you would at least let me know what happened when you got back there.'

Thomas carried on looking at her, seeming puzzled now. 'What do you mean?'

'I should have looked after Ada better, or not convinced the others to stay right from the start. It was all a mistake.'

'Ada doesn't think so, despite her accident,' Thomas said. 'She told me so. And Jean and Connie don't regret it either.'

'Don't they?'

'They're worried about their futures, of course, but I heard Connie say to Jean, 'What will we do now?' and Jean said, 'I don't know but aren't you glad we've got this to look back on?' and Connie said, 'You're right, not everyone has an experience like this in their lives' and they hugged one another and promised to stay in touch.'

Thomas stroked her cheek and went on, 'You didn't cause Ada's accident, Emma, but you gave her the chance to change, I'm sure.' He paused. 'And you and me, Emma — didn't it give us the freedom to say things, and do things, it would have taken us a year to get around to if we had stayed here? Did I do wrong to think you wanted to continue the way we'd started?'

'When we parted outside the inn that morning you didn't look at me or touch me. You didn't even look back and wave. I thought I'd lost you because I'd ruined it all.'

'Oh, Emma. I was so afraid of showing what I felt in front of Ada and your brother, I couldn't so much as look at you.' He reached up to touch her hair. 'Ada felt so bad already.'

He looked so distressed Emma wondered why she had ever doubted his love. She put her arms around Thomas again and he held her close for a moment before she lifted her head again for another kiss, slower and deeper than before so Emma felt as though she was melting.

Nothing had changed. Why did she think anything would be different between her and Thomas just because nothing else was the same? He was her constant and the miracle was he looked to her to be his constant. And no one blamed her for the way it ended at Mitchfield.

It was a while before she had enough control of her voice to ask, 'What happened at Mitchfield?'

Thomas sighed. 'When I got back to

the house there was a letter from Mrs Turner telling us to close the house and come back.'

'They hadn't read it, had they, Jean and Connie?' Emma asked.

'No. Now I see why you didn't let me ask Jean to write to Mrs Honey the day we left. Sorry I didn't understand at the time. They had an idea the letter might be asking them to come back so they started the washing. They thought it would be an excuse to stay another week — and anyway it had to be done as part of the spring clean.'

'That was a good idea, just to have a little more time to think and plan properly.'

'I thought so too,' Thomas said. 'I offered to write back to Mrs Turner and we discussed what to say, then Jean and Connie both signed the letter explaining we needed a few more days as we couldn't leave wet washing in a closed house.'

'She shouldn't have been able to argue with that,' Emma mused.

'You'd think not,' Thomas said. 'There was another letter the next day — Mrs Turner wouldn't have got ours yet — saying Jean and Connie should close the house and go back to their own homes. They were dismissed, Emma, just like that.'

'In a letter,' Emma said. 'That's so unfair.'

'I was to bring the accounts book back to the Hall,' Thomas went on, 'and anything missing would come out of their wages, which would be forwarded to them — if there was any, she wrote.'

'That's concerning, Thomas. Mrs Turner is capable of fixing it so there is a lot missing,' Emma said. 'She's making me pay for my uniform because I left my things behind at Mitchfield.'

'I brought them back, you know, Emma — Kitty ran them up to your room.'

'Thank you.' Emma lifted her cheek and rubbed it against Thomas's. It was rough against her smooth cheek and as she thought of the contrast between their hands Thomas lifted his smooth hands to her face, held it for a moment and then kissed her oh so gently, awakening in her feelings she wondered how she could ever contain.

Thomas was silent for a moment, then went on, 'I didn't ever think I'd see Jean cry, but she couldn't help herself. They both did, and I admit I shed a tear as well over the injustice of it. I even wrote to Mr Sewell to see if he could intervene but he didn't answer.'

'But you stayed to finish the laundry?'

'We couldn't leave it wet even hanging in the drying room. So we finished it and put it all away, made the rest of the house as good as we could and wrote a long note to explain all we'd done.'

'Mrs Moss never appeared again, then?'

'No.' Thomas shook his head. 'She'll get a shock next time she turns up there.'

'If she ever does,' Emma said. 'So much for keeping an eye on us.' She thought for a moment. 'I don't know quite where Jean and Connie both live but it's not near Mitchfield. They didn't have to walk all the way, did they?'

'No, we managed to hire a carriage each for them to get home. There was nowhere in Lexford that did that so it took quite a lot of enquiring but I couldn't have them going alone and they didn't want to either.'

'I should think not.' Emma was still indignant for her friends.

'Before they left I made them divide up the rest of the food to take with them. We left that larder empty.' He made a grim little laugh. 'Oh, Emma,' he added. 'In a minute will you go through the accounts book with me to make sure it's right? I don't want anything to be missing, and I've got the money that's left over. Will you help me make sure it tallies?'

'Of course I will,' Emma said heartily. 'And as for the food, I'm glad Jean and Connie didn't go empty-handed to their families.'

'Then we closed the house and each went our separate ways,' Thomas finished. 'More tears were shed, Emma, I can tell you. This shouldn't have been how it ended.'

'Have you spoken to Mr Sewell since you've been back?'

'He won't see me,' Thomas said bitterly. 'He won't even look me in the eye. I promised Connie and Jean I'd speak to him about contacting Mrs Honey to get a character for them both but it looks like that won't work either.'

'He may still listen to you,' Emma said. 'Although he does look grey and ill these days.'

'Oh, and I went to see Ada on the way through. Her parents are that angry about the way she was dismissed . . . '

'I can imagine. How is Ada?'

'The swelling is going down slowly and there's no fever. She sends you her best, Emma. They all speak highly of you.' He pressed her to him again. 'Oh, and Jimmy passed by to see us when he got back to let us know Ada had got home safely and you'd gone on to see Mrs Honey.'

'Oh, that's good, he got home safely.'

'I do like your brother, Emma, and admire him. He's making his own chances. Well, you do that as well but you keep doubting yourself.'

'*Is* it all my fault? Did I take charge and make you all stay and do the spring clean when it would have been more sensible to come back?'

'I wasn't there on the first day, but I don't think even you could have persuaded Jean to do something she didn't want to, and Connie would have followed Jean's lead and come back. And if I had been there, I would have agreed we get on with the job we'd been sent to do.'

'I liked myself better when I thought we were achieving something there,' Emma said. 'It doesn't feel like such an achievement now.'

She leaned into him and he hugged her a little tighter. 'It was,' he said.

'You'll see later.'

'I'm glad we're together, Thomas,' Emma said.

'So am I. This is a bad situation, but everything's better when you're there.'

18

Emma felt the same as Thomas — everything was better when he was there. But in truth they weren't really together. Monica watched Emma like a hawk and didn't allow her to stay up again, whatever the state of her stockings. To be truthful Emma was too tired most evenings to wait for Thomas or for the chance to catch up with William, even if it would be the only friendly contact of the day.

It was already the beginning of September and Emma began to feel, earlier in the year than usual, a degree of dread for the winter. The dark mornings when the washing water had turned solid and the insides of the windows were coated with a thin layer of ice. In her room, getting dressed meant your teeth chattered through the first three layers of clothing and you shivered your way through the rest of the ritual.

She wondered if Monica would stay with her once it got so cold, or if she would be able to contrive a better room from Mrs Turner. She suspected the viciousness of the woman was such that she'd suffer herself just for the pleasure of seeing Emma suffer.

However, one day there was an announcement at morning prayers that caused an excited ripple through the assembled servants. There was to be a fair in the village — and they would be allowed to go. As they left, Emma couldn't help noticing that Mrs Turner looked furious — even more than usual. She wondered if she had opposed the day out for her staff and been overruled by the family.

As it was, there was a list of things they could and couldn't do when they were out, including the male and female staff mixing.

Kitty laughed about that in their snatched moment the next morning. 'No, that's not Turner,' she said. 'That was the rule last year as well but once you're out, they can't enforce it!'

'Does the fair happen every year?'

'Yes. They take over the land past the church and all the way along that end of the thoroughfare towards the other big house.' Emma hadn't seen Kitty excited since she'd been back. 'It was good last year, Emma — there was music and dancing and sweets and a coconut shy . . . '

'Do you think I might be able to go and see Ada?' Emma asked. 'While the fair's on?'

'You'd have to keep an eye on the time but you probably could get away,' Kitty said. Thinking, she added, 'Although I reckon if they have to put Ada in a wheelbarrow and wheel her round, they'll be there — all of them.' She laughed. 'Everyone goes to the fair!'

Emma smiled as she ran back to her chores. That was something to look forward to and some time alone — even alone in a crowd — with Thomas. She was determined it would be fun.

'Emma, you will get up early on the morning of the fair to sweep the family living rooms,' Monica told Emma two days before the fair.

'I thought the family were leaving tomorrow,' Emma said. She was sometimes too sleepy to listen to Mr Sewell's mumbled announcements. She regretted the words as soon as they were out as Monica's face turned to thunder.

'Are you saying you're too lazy to do your job properly when the family are away? The girl who boasts of doing the spring cleaning of a big house alone? I hope someone goes soon to inspect your work and sees it for what it is.'

'No, Monica.' Emma cast her eyes down as she spoke. 'Of course I'll do my job.'

'I would hope so. Anyone found wanting these next few days won't go to the fair.'

Emma went back to work worried. It would be so easy for them to prevent any one of them from going just on a whim.

She cast her mind back to what William had told her. Miss Elizabeth was staying with her godmother and would be there for a couple of weeks. His Lordship and Her Ladyship were going to Sussex. There had been talk of William going as well but he'd been relieved it was decided he wouldn't need to. He didn't like all the dogs in that household.

Both he and Thomas could go to the fair, he said. But he'd felt the atmosphere as well.

'Don't put a foot wrong, Emma. Turner wants an excuse for us not to go.'

'She can't watch us all every minute of the day when we're out.'

'She probably could. She's like one of those insects with eyes that see all the way round them at the same time.' William laughed, and Emma did too. 'But she's not coming with us,' he added. 'She's taking the chance to go and visit her family, so she says. And Mr Sewell is meeting his brother at the inn. It'll only be Monica the Monster we'll have to look out for!'

★ ★ ★

Monica was closeted with Mrs Turner the next night when Emma managed to snatch a moment to sit down. Most of the others had gone to bed, some of them muttering about how much time Monica spent in the housekeeper's room.

'I don't understand it,' Kitty had said, after looking around to make sure Peggy and Sarah were not listening. 'Mrs Turner's old enough to be Monica's mother.'

Emma laughed. 'Fancy having her as a mother!'

She was hoping for the chance to see William or Thomas. Fortunately they were both in the servants' hall cleaning their shoes. William got up to go but she stopped him.

'Don't go, William. We've probably

only got a minute before Monica comes out and anyway I'm dead on my feet. I'm determined to get a good night's sleep before tomorrow. Did the family leave all right?'

'It was odd, Emma,' William said and Thomas nodded as if encouraging him to tell the story. 'His Lordship was in such a strange mood. I'm standing there with his jacket and he's debating with Mr Sewell about whether to take his pocket watch or not.' William sat down again but started gathering his things together. 'He was worried about losing it. I didn't see how he could lose it at his daughter's house but he eventually gave it back to Mr Sewell to put away for him.'

'That wasn't the strangest thing, though, was it?' Thomas put in.

'No, because then they start to make the arrangements for after. 'Miss Elizabeth will be here the day after tomorrow,' he says. 'You will look after her, won't you, Sewell?' and Mr Sewell is nodding, 'Yes, my lord, yes, my lord' as if he knew it all beforehand.'

'I don't think Monica knows Miss Elizabeth's coming back early,' Emma said. 'She would have lined someone up to attend to her if she had.' She stopped. 'Unless Miss Elizabeth is bringing someone with her.'

'Mr Sewell was happier than I've seen him in a while today,' Thomas added. 'He must be looking forward to seeing his brother tomorrow.'

There was a sound at the housekeeper's door and Emma got up to go. 'Wait for me tomorrow, Thomas,' she said as she left. 'We can go to the fair together.'

'It's going to be a good day,' Thomas said.

Her last image of Thomas as she fled upstairs was the crinkle at the edge of his eyes that denoted a special smile just for her.

*   *   *

The next morning Monica woke her up early and hurried Emma to get on with her work. Kitty wasn't down yet and Emma knew she would have plenty of time, but she didn't mind and completed her tasks as well as ever.

It had rained in the night but the sun was now appearing through the clouds, and it promised to be another fine dry day.

'Monica's left,' Kitty told her. 'But she said you're to clean 'her' room before you go.'

'Nooo,' Emma groaned.

'It'll be all right, everyone's got extra to do after breakfast so we're going an hour later. It won't be properly started yet anyway. We're all going to get changed and meet down here.'

'Where's Monica gone, do you know?' Emma asked. 'To the fair already?'

'She didn't say,' Kitty said cheerfully. 'I expect she's going to hide somewhere and leap out at us if we behave improperly!' She laughed.

Emma swept the floor of the bedchamber and washed the surfaces, then took the water down to the scullery. No one was assembled yet so she went up to get changed. She looked at her bed. *I can just lie down for five minutes*, she mused as, despite her excitement, her eyes closed.

★ ★ ★

The next thing Emma knew was that Kitty was shaking her and saying, 'Wake up, Emma. Where is Thomas? Wake up!'

Emma's head felt fuzzy with sleep and she was slow to wake up.

'Thomas? He's waiting for me downstairs to go to the fair. I'll change quickly and get down.'

'Emma, what are you talking about? The fair's over and nobody's seen Thomas all day!'

Emma shook her head to clear it. Perhaps it was true — the light was fading outside. So she had missed her day out. And now she had to go down and find out what else had happened.

19

Emma was wide awake by the time she got down to the servants' hall. Mr Sewell was sitting at the head of the table. To his right, William was speaking . . .

'The jewellery has been taken from the cases and the empty cases left open for all to see,' he said. 'It was a hurried job.'

Emma noticed that many of the outdoor staff were there too. She recognised the head gardener and Eric. Kitty now entered and went to sit by Eric. 'The medal case has been forced open,' she said, clearly upset. 'They're all gone.'

'And His Lordship's valuables?' Mr Sewell asked William. 'Gone too?'

William nodded. Mr Sewell looked downcast for a moment, then he turned his eyes to Emma and as she met them for a split second she saw something determined in them.

'Emma, you didn't go to the fair,' he said.

'No, sir. I went up to change ready to go and lay down for a moment and must have fallen asleep. I've only just woken up.'

'You were friendly with Mr Hedges — Thomas — weren't you?'

Were? Emma didn't think this was a time to ask questions. She'd get the whole story from William later if she didn't pick it up now. 'Yes,' was all she said.

She was questioned over and over. What time did she sleep? After breakfast and once she had cleaned her room. Where was Thomas at that time? She didn't know. Did she hear any noise in the house during the day? No, you don't hear anything up in the attic. Had she spoken to Thomas this morning? No. Did she know what he was planning? No.

After a while Emma formed a picture

of what they were saying. Thomas had crept around the house stealing jewellery and medals while she slept and then made off with them!

How could anyone possibly believe that?

'Emma, I have to ask you again,' Mr Sewell insisted. 'Did you know what Thomas was planning?'

'He was planning to go to the fair with me,' she said. 'He was going to wait for me so we could go together.'

'Do you have any idea where he is now, where he would go?'

'No. Mr Sewell, if you think he stole from the family, you're mistaken.'

It was a risk talking to Mr Sewell like that but Monica and Mrs Turner weren't there and no one else was speaking up for Thomas.

Mr Sewell looked at her. 'I very much hope I am, Emma,' he said. 'But I don't see any other explanation.'

Further down the table Eric the under gardener cleared his throat. 'There are footprints in the flower beds outside the back door,' he said. 'And a muddy footprint on the floor in the kitchen.'

Mr Sewell looked at him. 'And?'

'It's smaller than Thomas's, sir. Thomas and William both have quite big feet. Someone else was in the kitchen.'

Mr Sewell got up. 'William, come with me. Are your feet a similar size to Thomas's?'

'Yes, sir. Our shoes are the same size.'

Kitty was looking at Eric admiringly.

'But where is Thomas?' Cook asked as the two men left. 'There could well have been outsiders come in but it looks bad that he's hopped it along with the valuables.'

'Where are Monica and Mrs Turner?' Emma countered. 'They could just as easily have come back and done it.' She wondered if Eric had looked at the size of their feet as well.

'And Thomas gone with them?' Cook said.

No, that was even less likely.

So where was Thomas?

Emma sat with William after Mr Sewell had sent everyone to bed and trudged wearily up himself.

'Poor Mr Sewell,' William said. 'He didn't have a good time at the fair either. His brother's son, Silas, runs the inn at our end of the village and has got himself into some trouble or another. I think they spent the whole day discussing it.'

'And you, William? Did you have a good time?'

William's tense face softened. 'I did. I won a prize for Flora on the coconut shy. She thinks I'm something special and, do you know, when I'm with her I can be.' He laughed at himself. 'But now I think I should have waited for Thomas,' William added. 'I left him here because I was keen to go and meet Flora.'

'Of course you were. And I shouldn't have let myself fall asleep.'

'You don't think he could have been

planning this all along, do you?' William asked.

Emma had been asking herself this question and her conviction of Thomas's honesty wavered a little more at the thought that even William could suspect him.

'No,' she said finally. 'He showed me the accounts book from Mitchfield House — I'd started making a really detailed record of every farthing we spent and he carried it on after I left. Then on the last day he sent Connie and Jean home in carriages to be sure they'd get to their families safely, but he walked back here and slept in the open air instead of the inn to save the housekeeping money.' She felt tears coming and blinked them back. 'Once he got here, he made me count the money that was left and make sure it all tallied with the accounts book. I can't believe he's got any dishonesty in him, William.'

'Nor me,' William agreed. 'It's a mystery.'

'This is as bad as it can be, isn't it? We never found out what happened to Lily and I don't see how we're going to solve this one either.'

★　★　★

Monica didn't return that night and Emma's hope grew that she and Mrs Turner would be found responsible for the robbery. Perhaps they'd kidnapped Thomas because he saw them. She didn't pursue the imagining much further because she believed either of them to be capable of murder, which would make more sense than kidnapping. And there was Eric's theory relating to the muddy footprint that didn't fit that scene.

'How did Thomas seem when you left him yesterday?' she asked Kitty in the morning.

'Happy,' she said. 'We all were, even Mr Sewell. He was keen to get off so we all went and he left Thomas the key to lock up.'

'There, Mr Sewell wouldn't have done that if he didn't think Thomas was trustworthy.'

'We left Thomas sitting at the table in our parlour with the key on the table. I noticed it was in the same place when I got back, but I wasn't the first one back.'

'Who was, do you know?'

'Mr Sewell, I think. He was doing his usual nightly round when he saw the medal case open.'

'I hope Mrs Turner and Monica don't come back today,' Emma said. 'I'd like to go and ask in the village if anyone saw Thomas. He'd have to go that way if he went anywhere.'

'Beyond the church, it was so busy anyone could have seen him.'

'It would still be safer than going across the fields, though, if you've got stolen jewellery in your pocket,' Emma said. 'Anyone from the farms could see you and stop you. And there's no way through the other way, is there?'

She knew she was right. Going in the

other direction would be very unlikely. Apart from paths to the two farms the trail led only to a house that had not been inhabited for many years and had fallen into extreme disrepair. No one local remembered when the owner had last been there or indeed who it was. It would be the third generation of heirs who would come to claim it now and why would they? It was worthless, or at least more would have to be spent on it to make it habitable than it was worth. After that house, there was no road to speak of and walking the hills and forests beyond would be daunting even for a desperate criminal.

'That's what Eric said,' Kitty agreed. 'We talked some more outside after everyone went to bed. He reckons if the thief was on foot they'd go up past the inn on our side, cut across the church-yard and around the edge of the fields there. There would have been one or two people going to or coming from the fair so it wouldn't provoke notice and none of us would be there.'

'And then where would he go?'

Kitty shrugged. 'Anywhere. Unless you were in a horse and cart, Eric said. Then you could hide the jewellery in the back and go straight through town and no one would know.'

'Eric thinks Thomas had accomplices in a horse and cart?'

'He thought he saw the marks of wheels and hooves as we came back. He wondered who from the farms beyond us would have taken their cart to the fair. But, when we were talking after, he thought whoever did the robbery may have come in a horse and cart.'

'He should tell Mr Sewell.'

'If we're questioned he will, but it's supposition and doesn't explain where Thomas is.'

'By the way, Kitty, I heard Miss Elizabeth is coming back today. Did anyone ask you to attend to her, with water for her bath and so on?'

'No, nobody said anything,' Kitty said. 'But I can be ready. I'm getting to like Miss Elizabeth more — she's lost that hardness she had about her and I get a 'thank you, Kitty' lately. Anyway, so long as it's not the Earl, I'll take water to anyone.'

★ ★ ★

By the time Emma finished her early morning chores Monica and Mrs Turner were back and everything seemed back to normal. Except nothing was normal, because the robbery and Thomas's absence were on everyone's minds.

After breakfast Mr Sewell called Emma and William into his parlour. This earned him a look like thunder from Mrs Turner but she couldn't prevent it.

'Emma has work to do, Mr Sewell,' was all she said.

'There are more pressing things, Mrs Turner,' the butler returned.

Once seated behind his desk Mr Sewell looked at them both. 'This is a to-do,' he said. 'Whether Thomas was involved in this theft or not, the thing to do now is to find him. Do you not have any idea where he would go?' he asked desperately.

'I think wherever he went, he did not go willingly,' Emma said.

Mr Sewell looked at her appraisingly. 'Yes. I dare say you're right.'

Buoyed by this comment, Emma went on, 'I would like, with your permission, to ask the locals if they saw anything yesterday. It may give us an idea who was here and where they went.'

Mr Sewell sighed. 'I don't suppose it will help but I need to be able to tell His Lordship no stone was left unturned. I fear he will mourn the loss of his pocket watch for its sentimental value.'

'Do I have your permission, then?' Emma asked. 'I'm afraid Mrs Turner would not approve.'

'Yes, my authority is above hers in this. Go, and you too, William, and find out what you can.'

William hesitated. 'I'm happy to go, sir, but do you forget Miss Elizabeth will return today? Should I not be here to greet her?'

'I should be the one to do that, thank you. She'll have a proper greeting.'

'Kitty is ready to answer her bell, should she need anything, Mr Sewell,' Emma said.

'Good, good,' the butler said. 'Does everyone downstairs know of her arrival?'

'No, just Kitty.'

'Mrs Turner does not need to know yet,' Mr Sewell told them. 'Or the upper housemaid.'

Emma nodded. She most certainly wasn't going to tell Monica or Mrs Turner. 'Will you authorise my absence, then?' she asked.

He sighed again. 'I will steel myself to go and speak to Mrs Turner.' He looked solemn but surely there was a twinkle in his eye.

Mr Sewell was in charge again, and she and William were going to do some detective work. They'd find Thomas and all would be fine.

20

As the door closed on yet another household that had been at the fair and seen nothing, William said, 'I suppose we're lucky Mr Sewell is letting us go around asking for information. We're not getting any, but at least we're trying.'

They'd run up to the folly before going to the village, in the vain hope Thomas may be there for some reason, but it was empty. They hadn't been surprised but William was right — they were trying everything they could think of.

'Mr Sewell blames himself, doesn't he?' Emma said. 'I'm sorry we haven't found anything out for him. It'll be dark soon.'

William looked at the sky. 'Just these last few cottages, then.'

Emma knocked at the next door.

'There was a robbery at Lewin Hall yesterday while the fair was on,' she explained to the householder. 'Did you happen to see anything?'

'Come in and ask Grandfather. He stayed behind at home.'

Grandfather couldn't move fast but there was nothing wrong with his eyes, or his mind.

'A horse and cart came by not long after you all passed by on your way to the fair.' He looked at Emma. 'I didn't see you with them.'

'I didn't manage to get to the fair,' Emma told him, impressed by his powers of observation. 'Who was driving the cart?'

'Two men. Not from the village.' He turned to his son. 'Those two who cause trouble.'

'The ones who hurt poor Mary Ann that time?' the man's son asked.

The grandfather nodded. 'Mary Ann was out as well yesterday. I saw her hide from them.'

'Did you happen to see what was in

the cart?' William asked.

The man shook his head. 'Straw and rags,' he said with a shrug.

They questioned the man a little more but he had no information and would not be drawn into supposition, which was a blessing. They thanked him heartily and left.

'Mary Ann,' Emma said once they were outside and had turned their steps towards the Hall again. 'That's the woman Thomas helped that day, isn't it? Have we time to go and see her?'

Emma wondered if she would be able to question Mary Ann about Lily as well, or secure permission to return another day and see her. If Mrs Turner ever allowed her out again after today.

It was already getting dark by the time they reached the tiny cottage. It was away from the main thoroughfare, off the beaten track, as Thomas had indicated. It was quite isolated between trees and shrubs.

'I wonder how she manages, living here on her own,' Emma wondered.

'If she uses herbs and plants for healing she has easy access to plenty here,' William said.

They glanced around carefully. There were any number of places to hide and watch. It felt as though invisible eyes were on them from all directions. They knocked on the door, softly at first so as not to startle anyone inside, but then louder as the door remained firmly closed.

Emma was sure she heard a sound inside. A sound as of a cat mewing or some other small animal. The walls and door of the cottage were surprisingly thick and it was difficult to tell if there was movement and voices within or not.

'Hello,' Emma called. 'We work at the Hall and are looking for our friend. You know him.'

Emma was sure she heard a conversation just inside the door but couldn't make out any words. 'Please talk to us,' she added.

Someone opened the door a crack. She was a woman in her forties in a woollen dress and a shawl around her shoulders, over which her wavy dark hair tumbled. She visibly jumped when she saw William. 'Are you his brother?' she asked.

'No. I'm a footman with him.'

Mary Ann, if that was who she was, closed the door. Emma thought she heard voices again inside but it still wasn't clear and she was reluctant to put her ear to the door in case it opened again. When it did open the woman thrust a bag at them.

'Take this,' she said and closed the door.

No matter how much they knocked and called she didn't open it again and they heard no more voices or animal noises.

★ ★ ★

The valuables lay on Mr Sewell's table. He moved them into piles as he checked what came out of the bag against the inventory the staff had made while Emma and William had been out.

'Well done, well done,' he kept saying, relief evident in his face. He took the grubby bag up again and looked inside, then shook it out.

'Is something missing?' William asked.

'His Lordship's pocket watch.' The butler had gone pale.

'Is it very valuable?' Emma asked.

'Well, his mother gave it to him just before she died.' The butler looked up from the table and shook his head. 'So it is irreplaceable.'

★ ★ ★

By next morning Emma had decided she would ask Mr Sewell if she could go back to the cottage in the forest. She was afraid the two ruffians were using Mary Ann against her will, although she was unsure what she could do about it if it proved true. Mr Sewell would know what to do. At the very least Mary Ann may know what had happened to His Lordship's pocket watch. If they could only get that back. And she might know what had happened to Thomas.

She spoke to Kitty to tell her of her idea, but Kitty stopped her at the mention of permission to go out again. 'Mr Sewell was taken ill in the night,' Kitty said. 'The physician was called.'

'Oh, poor man! Do you know what's wrong?'

The other maid shook her head. 'William says he heard a thump as he was on his way to bed and found him on the floor, not able to move one side of him. He couldn't talk because that side of his face didn't work. William was frightened and woke the hall boy to run for the physician.'

'I don't know whether to run out now, before Monica and Mrs Turner are up, or risk trying to get away later,' Emma said, indecisive.

'It's a risk, Emma. Are you sure you want to do it without authority? You could lose your job.'

'I know he'd give permission if he was well.'

'That wouldn't be enough for Mrs Turner.'

'No,' Emma reflected. 'Now would be the safest time to go but it's very early to be calling on someone.'

'It is, Emma. Suppose you went instead of breakfast and prayers?'

'That I could do,' Emma said thoughtfully.

'Hurry through your morning chores,' Kitty said. 'I'll bring a piece of bread out to the front and bring your cloths in so you can run the moment you're supposed to be outside doing the steps.'

'Would you, Kitty?'

'But that's all I can do. I won't tell where you are but I won't be able to do anything else. I don't have your courage, Emma.'

'That's all right, Kitty, I understand,' Emma said. 'I don't really have much courage either. I'm doing it for Thomas, like you'd do it for Eric.'

True to her word, Kitty flew out to the front the second Emma was there. She thrust the bread at Emma and grabbed her cleaning materials, obviously terrified. 'Stay safe,' she muttered.

Emma knew if she hesitated she wouldn't go. She didn't have the courage Kitty thought she did. She lifted her skirts and ran. She was doing this for Thomas — but for Mr Sewell now as well.

Emma didn't know if she was more afraid of being stopped by Mrs Turner than of what would happen if she encountered the two ruffians or someone else stopped and challenged her, but she reached the street leading to the village with no problem. The few farmers and labourers about only nodded or took no notice. She was a maid in a hurry to find an article for her master's breakfast or to take an urgent message for him.

As she neared Mary Ann's cottage, she instinctively took cover. The house stood in its own clearing but there were trees and shrubs to hide her only a short distance away. Wasn't Mary Ann fearful of being watched from the forest?

There was no movement while she

watched and waited for her heartbeat to return to its normal speed. She felt paralysed but knew she had to move. Emma approached the cottage gingerly and listened carefully to see if anyone was inside.

Heartened by the silence, she peered through the window. It was none too clean, she noticed. A sudden movement inside made her duck down quickly, her legs shaking too much to run.

As the door slowly opened and she saw a tall male form appear in the shadow of the door Emma looked around for something to protect herself with and picked up a branch. It was too thin to do any damage, but Emma wasn't sure whether she'd be able to hurt anyone even if she was in fear for her life. Then the man spoke.

'Emma? What are you doing here?'

★ ★ ★

Thomas expertly mixed her a potion he told her Mary Ann said was calming. As she drank it, the whole story of why she was there came out.

All the time she was watching Thomas, looking so handsome despite obviously having slept for two nights in the same clothes, but with a large wound on his forehead.

Once the tale was out and it was clear she couldn't answer any questions about Mr Sewell she couldn't contain her own curiosity any more.

'Thomas, what happened to you?'

Thomas reached up and touched the wound on his forehead. 'I was waiting for you to go to the fair. Everyone else had left and when I heard a noise outside, I thought it was one of them come back. But two men walked in the open back door and without a word hit me.'

Emma gasped but resisted the temptation to reach out for Thomas. Mary Ann could be back any moment.

'When I woke up,' Thomas went on, 'I was in a moving cart with a bag of the family's valuables beside me. Where were you, Emma?'

'Oh, Thomas,' Emma cried. 'I fell asleep! I didn't mean to but I closed my eyes for five minutes and didn't wake until everyone was back from the fair and you'd gone!'

He smiled. 'Poor Emma. You were so tired. I thought you didn't want to go to the fair with me.'

'Of course I did! But how did you get away?'

There was a soft sound at the door and Thomas shot up, steadying himself as he rose too fast. 'I need to tell Mary Ann there's someone here,' he said. 'She's not used to visitors.'

Thomas seemed to take Mary Ann a bit further outside to talk to her because she could hear soft murmuring but not what was said. It sounded like three voices, Thomas's and two different females but she didn't know the tone of Mary Ann's yet and she was still somewhat agitated by her experience.

She looked around the little cottage, having so far only had eyes for Thomas.

The hearth dominated the tiny room and was hung with herbs and flowers, most of which Emma had no names for. Their scent perfumed the air. It was a little overpowering, she thought, but perhaps you got used to it.

There was a little scullery to one side and through the half open door Emma could see laundry hanging up to dry. Some shawls and some tiny garments Emma couldn't identify from this distance. She was about to get up and go for a better look when she noticed the basket in the corner, surely set up as a baby's crib. Her mother had used just such a basket for her youngest when he was born early. Mary Ann had a baby!

21

Emma felt a sudden sympathy for the woman she didn't know. How hard it must be for Mary Ann to be alone with a baby in this place. Unless, of course, there was a husband? Emma was still speculating when Mary Ann herself came hurrying in, hands outstretched to Emma and not at all shy of company.

'Emma, my dear. I saw you yesterday but we didn't want anyone to see Thomas, not just yet. We were afraid the parish constable would be looking for him to take him to prison.'

'No one has called the constable — at least, not yet,' Emma said.

'That is good, for no one believes the constable serves the interests of justice,' Mary Ann said.

'Thank you for looking after Thomas,' Emma said. She turned to him again. 'But how did you come to be here?'

'Ah, I was just telling you,' Thomas said. 'After I came to in the cart and realised I was all covered up and on the move, I had a good listen and could hear two voices up front, so I stayed put for a while. Then the cart stopped and everything went quiet. I looked out to see where we were, and it was outside the inn. I could hear the two voices fading in the distance so I risked getting out. I just grabbed the bag and jumped out. It was a good job Mary Ann was there because I made myself so dizzy jumping I would have swooned on the path and they'd probably have come out and finished me off.'

Mary Ann smiled. She had a gentle smile and Emma took to her.

'So you brought him back here to your home?' Emma asked.

'It took us a long time, didn't it, Thomas?' she said, then turned back to Emma. 'I left him on the floor just inside the door for several hours before I could move him somewhere comfortable. An unconscious man is a dead weight.' She laughed. 'Fortunately with a bit of tending, he recovered from his wound as well as my lack of care in dragging him along.'

'It's a wonder you got me here at all,' Thomas said. 'Mary Ann is stronger than she looks.'

It was on the tip of Emma's tongue to say, 'And so soon delivered of a baby,' but there was no baby with Mary Ann and no sound of it in the cottage. Surely a mother would go to her infant the minute she got home? Perhaps the baby had died. That would be dreadful. She could not mention it. And there was certainly no husband, or he surely would have helped move Thomas.

But Mary Ann spoke again of the day of the fair.

'There was something missing from the bag, wasn't there?' she asked. 'As I was watching from the side of the road, before Thomas jumped, I saw the two men take something into the inn that glinted gold.'

'Yes, His Lordship's pocket watch. I

hoped — as well as finding Thomas — to find it to take back. It would ease Mr Sewell's mind so much to have it returned.'

Mary Ann told her, 'The word in the village is that the innkeeper, Silas, is a go-between for those who steal and those who buy stolen property. He's a weak man and has been frightened into doing it by someone important who can prevent him continuing in his business if he doesn't cooperate. They wrecked his premises once and can do it again. Unless a buyer has been along already, Silas will still have the pocket watch.' She thought for a moment. 'His Lordship is important in the district. He could get it back.'

'He is away from home,' Emma said. 'And Mr Sewell, the butler at the Hall and Silas's uncle, is ill and I don't think he could get out to speak to his nephew today.'

Mary Ann stood up and it seemed to Emma to be a signal for her to go. 'I will try to find out who comes to buy the pocket watch but these things go through many hands to hide their provenance.'

Thomas stood up too. 'We know the important personage who was behind the robbery, Emma. He gave information to the two who carried it.'

'Who?' Emma asked.

'One who is behind practically all the criminal acts in this district,' Mary Ann said. 'And who manipulates justice. The Earl of Thorncombe.'

'Surely not!' Emma stuttered. Knowing he was an unsavoury man was not enough to believe he was involved in crime — and would actually steal from someone who had shown him hospitality, who had been a good friend of his father!

'Ask anyone in the village, Emma,' Mary Ann said. 'Or rather, do not ask them, because the fear of this man's influence runs high.'

Thomas walked Emma to the place in the forest where she would turn on to the barely marked path that would lead her to the main thoroughfare.

'Do you believe that about the Earl, Thomas?' she asked when they had left the cottage.

'I'm afraid I do,' he said. 'Being high born or having a title doesn't mean you are free of corruption and depravity.'

'He is not here very often,' Emma said.

'He stays nearby,' Thomas told her. 'His Lordship doesn't know.'

'People are saying he killed his father — could there be any truth in that?' Emma asked.

Thomas shrugged. 'He has many who do his bidding.' He seemed to be hurrying her along as if he wanted to be sure she was gone. He must have picked up Mary Ann's suspicious ways.

'Don't accompany me any further, Thomas. You must rest — and I fear someone will see you and report you.'

She reached up to give him a quick kiss and he took her face in his hands and held it tenderly as their lips met. She almost faltered and begged to stay with him in the quiet cottage. When they broke apart Emma avoided looking into Thomas's eyes because she knew she shouldn't linger any longer — and he shouldn't be out at all.

'I'll find a way to come again,' she said.

Thomas nodded. He slid his hand down her arm, touched her hand and turned immediately to go back to the cottage. Emma looked back once to see if he would turn to wave but he was going as fast as he could with the weakness his injury had left him. She saw him disappear and thought he'd gone in the door very quickly, but then she caught a glimpse of movement in the shrubs opposite the cottage.

Emma turned for a final time at the turn-off. Thomas and Mary Ann were both on the path to the cottage door and Mary Ann had her baby wrapped in her shawl.

Except it wasn't Mary Ann. The hair that streamed down her back was fair, not dark . . . fair, like Lily's.

A right turn at the end of the path that wasn't a path would take Emma back to the Hall.

She turned left.

So many thoughts crowded her brain she was not thinking at all. She certainly wasn't thinking enough to be afraid. There was too much to fear to put it into words in her head.

A woman was cleaning the outside windows of the inn. The surprising thought that crossed Emma's mind before she spoke was to wonder if Thomas would be able to clean Mary Ann's windows for her before he left. Her thoughts so often led her back to the time at Mitchfield House when everything changed.

Suddenly came the knowledge, beyond a shadow of a doubt, who the father of Lily's child was! That was another of the crimes Mary Ann had meant — and it would have been why Lily had had to leave when she knew he was going to be visiting again.

So that was why Lily had stopped talking. Emma would do whatever it took to get this man brought to justice — not so that Lily could benefit financially, because she didn't think that would happen, but simply for the sake of fairness.

'Is Silas inside?' she asked the woman.

The woman ceased her cleaning. 'Are you from the Hall?' she asked. 'Is it about his uncle?'

Emma stood there, not understanding.

'They sent word that his uncle had had a turn in the night,' the woman said. 'He hasn't . . . ?'

'I have no further news,' Emma said. 'But I would like to speak to Silas.'

'Go in.' The woman, probably Silas's wife, Emma thought, guided her into the inn and to a small room on the other side of the main public part. 'It's someone from the Hall to see you, Silas,' she called. 'But there's no news.'

They sat her down and offered her a drink.

'Have you seen my uncle?' Silas asked.

'No. The person who saw him this morning said one side of his face isn't working and he can't talk.' She lowered her voice, although there was no one else at the inn. 'He was very worried about the robbery and especially about losing His Lordship's pocket watch. He felt responsible.'

Silas nodded. 'He is loyal to Lord Lewin.' Silas looked very unhappy and uncomfortable.

'Have you got it?' Emma asked. 'I thought if I could take it back it might aid his recovery.'

Silas hesitated. 'My uncle knows the danger I'm in. The two who stole from His Lordship are in the employ of someone who could ruin me and has threatened to harm my family.'

'I know this, but I understand His Lordship has power over that person. Mr Sewell could ask him to intervene on your behalf, I'm sure.'

She wasn't sure. Perhaps if you pretended hard enough it came to pass despite your doubts.

'You're a convincing speaker for one so young,' Silas said. 'Would that Lord Lewin could make those two rogues outside disappear. They are the tools of the person behind all this. They have even threatened my children.'

'Does the parish constable know about this?'

Silas gave a grim laugh. 'The constable has given power to a substitute who is well paid by the Earl of Th — .' He stopped short. 'Oh, I never meant to mention him! Please forget I spoke.'

So Mary Ann was right and there was no hope of help. 'I already knew it,' she said. 'Let me take the pocket watch to your uncle, to ask His Lordship to inform the Earl he took it back to avoid him being reported to the authorities.'

'The Earl has no fear of the authorities,' Silas said despondently.

Silas's wife had been silent so far, but now spoke. 'Do it, Silas,' she said. 'If we have His Lordship on our side, all this could end.'

Lord Lewin's name carried weight and after another minute Emma was outside the inn with the pocket watch lodged about her person, where it would not be seen.

The two unpleasant-looking men were loitering outside and approached her, coming close.

'What's your business, girl?' one asked.

'I brought a message from Lord Lewin,' she said. 'The butler is gravely ill over the loss of His Lordship's pocket watch and if he dies, whoever robbed the Hall will hang.'

'Hang?' one man said, looking uneasy now.

'Lord Lewin won't rest until these thieves are punished,' she said bravely.

Emma looked around for something to lean against to prevent the two ruffians from seeing she was shaking, but they were too far from the wall of the inn. When she glanced ahead again she saw one of the men had come closer, with a menacing look. If he had a knife she could be dead in an instant — and she didn't have the courage she was pretending to have.

'And if you kill me you'll be hanged even faster!' she said, pushing past with a courage she didn't know she possessed. 'You'd be better off getting away now and saving yourselves.'

They hesitated for an instant and Emma started to move away. She willed herself not to look back but after a moment she picked up her skirts and ran as fast as she could. Dignified it wasn't — but she wouldn't die here in the street without having seen Thomas again or talked to Lily.

Her steps only slowed when she was inside the gate of the Hall, out of breath and trembling. Now all she had to do was force herself into the presence of His Lordship once he got home. She had his pocket watch nestled within her dress. He would have to be the one to solve this now.

★ ★ ★

The closer she got to the Hall the more certain Emma became that she'd be leaving straight away and would have no chance to speak to His Lordship. Instead she would have to go home, dismissed without a character.

She hesitated before creeping in at the open door to the kitchen. Cook wouldn't go running to Mrs Turner but she might not protect her either. Emma determined that Kitty wouldn't be blamed, whatever happened. She couldn't save Jean and Connie, or Ada, but she'd save Kitty.

Kitty greeted her in a louder voice than usual. 'Ah, Emma, did you come down from Mr Sewell's room for a breath of air? We didn't see you.'

'How is the poor man?' Cook asked.

Emma hesitated.

'I expect you need to get straight back up there, don't you?' Kitty said. 'Do you need some more cool water? I'll come up with you and bring the bowl down to refresh it, shall I?'

'Yes. Thank you, Kitty.'

She gratefully followed Kitty to a

corridor she'd never been on before, to Mr Sewell's room.

'I didn't know where the room was either,' Kitty said softly. 'You've been in here all morning.'

'How can I ever thank you?'

Kitty shook her head. 'I should thank you,' she whispered. 'I've been thinking about you all morning. It's not just about Thomas. You make things happen, Emma. Everything you did at Mitchfield House and getting Ada home and getting the jewellery back. After you left this morning I decided I didn't want to be just someone who does and goes where they're told. We don't have many choices but I saw I could be brave if I had a mind to, in small ways.'

'You probably saved me my job.'

'And I made Mr Sewell more comfortable and I got Cook out of the doldrums and baking again. It makes you feel strong, doesn't it?'

Emma nodded. 'It does,' she said.

Kitty knocked and entered Mr Sewell's bedchamber, as though she'd done this several times before. She went across to the bowl of water on the table by the butler's bed and took it and when she left Emma sat down at the bedside.

'Hello, Mr Sewell,' she said softly. 'I've got a story to tell you.' She glanced around the darkened room, suddenly afraid that Monica or Mrs Turner were lurking in the shadows.

Mr Sewell focused his eyes on her with difficulty. 'No — one — here,' he said, each word seeming painful to get out. 'Tell.'

Emma left nothing out, pausing only when Kitty brought some cold water. Mr Sewell refused Emma's offer to cool his face with it, and she continued. She wasn't sure how much the poorly butler was able to understand. Once or twice his lips tried to form a word and she repeated what she'd said or tried to explain it better. At the end she stood up and turned away to retrieve the pocket watch from where she'd hidden it and she was almost sure he managed half a smile.

'Where shall I put it, Mr Sewell?' she asked.

She was exasperated that there was a noise at the door at that very moment. She sat down again and hid the pocket watch under her apron.

It was Kitty with a message from downstairs. 'Mrs Turner says you're to go for your dinner and I'm to see if Mr Sewell can eat some soup.'

'I don't think soup is a good idea,' Emma said softly. 'I've given him some water and it just dribbles down his chin.'

'Well, we'll have a go. He needs something.'

Emma took the part of her apron covering the watch, with the watch itself wrapped in it, in her hand and stood up.

'That question I asked, Mr Sewell. Do you have any ideas?'

Kitty looked surprised when Mr Sewell answered, as slowly and painfully as before. 'Honey,' he said. 'Tell Honey.'

Emma went downstairs, pleased she'd told her story but unsure how much he'd really understood. From his last words it seemed as though he didn't quite remember what had happened in the house and that Mrs Honey had gone. She slipped the pocket watch back inside her clothes.

By the time she got down to the basement she'd convinced herself he'd been trying to say His Lordship because that was what she was going to have to do — persuade the one person in the household who was least likely to agree to see her, when he returned, to listen to her story.

22

Mrs Turner appeared different. More subdued, Emma thought; perhaps she was fond of Mr Sewell after all. She was, if that were possible, gentle with Emma, who couldn't suppress the thought that she knew about Emma's morning escapade and was waiting to accuse her.

Dinner was over when she got down but Cook had kept some back and Mrs Turner came to sit beside Emma as she was finishing her food.

'I know you are fond of Mr Sewell,' she said. 'And we're all upset. But it doesn't mean you can decide what you'll do. I run the house, remember.'

'Yes, Mrs Turner.'

'No more taking yourself off to Mr Sewell's room, unless I ask you to.'

'No, Mrs Turner.'

The housekeeper went on, 'Miss Elizabeth arrived back unexpectedly yesterday so Kitty will attend her. She'll be mostly keeping to her chamber, I understand, but you will help Cook, as Kitty did, so she can attend Miss Elizabeth.'

'Yes, Mrs Turner.' *So I'll be under your watchful eye*, Emma thought.

After she'd left and the door to her parlour had closed, Kitty came in.

'She's got Peggy and Sarah taking it in turns to be up with poor Mr Sewell,' Kitty said bitterly. 'We only got away with saying you were up there all morning because Peggy spent all the time reading in her own room. Now Turner's had a word with them they're going to be reading in his room instead. They've opened the curtains and Sarah's moved the chair to the window so no one will be watching if he takes a turn for the worse.'

'Where's Monica?' Emma asked then.

'I don't know whether she's reading in her room as well or if she's gone out,' Kitty said. 'She does as she pleases and gets away with it.'

'And Miss Elizabeth's here?'

'Yes. She's being really nice. Emma, how did you get on this morning?'

There was the sound of voices on the stairs.

'I'll tell you all about it later. Kitty, do you think I could speak to Miss Elizabeth?'

'Today might not be good. She says her ma's coming back this afternoon. I don't think Mrs Turner knows.' Kitty laughed as she returned to the kitchen. 'And I'm not telling her.'

★ ★ ★

Kitty was becoming someone to be totally relied upon. She'd persuaded Cook — who was feeling decidedly down because of Mr Sewell's condition — to bake some tempting morsels for Miss Elizabeth who, Kitty told her, had little appetite, in order for there to be plenty to offer Her Ladyship when she arrived.

She'd also warned William to be prepared and not be taken by surprise when the front bell rang. So Her Ladyship was greeted properly and William, as he later explained, had long experience in not showing emotion but could not resist a smile as he took her travelling companion's cloak and bag.

'Have my things sent up, William,' Her Ladyship said. 'And take Mrs Honey's things to the best guest bedchamber.'

'Yes, Your Ladyship.'

'Then we'll take tea in the parlour.'

William couldn't resist a laugh as he ran down to the kitchen where Emma and Mrs Turner were.

'Her Ladyship's here with a guest,' he said. 'They would like tea in the parlour. Mrs Turner, you might want to cast an eye over the best guest room to make sure it's aired and fit for Her Ladyship's visitor.'

'Goodness!' Mrs Turner said. 'Why couldn't she have warned us? Is it an important visitor?'

Emma noticed that William didn't answer until Mrs Turner had run upstairs. Then he turned to Emma and Cook. 'It's Mrs

Honey!' he mouthed.

'Mercy!' Cook said. 'Taking tea with Her Ladyship! And Mrs Turner rushing to make the room ready for an important visitor.'

★　★　★

After the tea went up Emma hovered nervously in the kitchen with Kitty and Cook, ready to take over Kitty's duties preparing dinner when Miss Elizabeth rang and Kitty would have to go up and help her.

'Could I collect the tray from the parlour when they ring for it to be removed?' she asked. 'I'd like to ask to talk to them.'

'What's going on?' Cook asked suspiciously.

'I'll tell you eventually — but I have to tell Her Ladyship first,' Emma said.

'Do you know something about young Thomas and the robbery?' Cook continued.

It would be such a relief to tell Cook everything, hand over the pocket watch

— it was beginning to feel very heavy against her person — but she was afraid if she didn't tell the story direct to Her Ladyship and Mrs Honey, it would change in the passing from mouth to mouth and once there were misunderstandings they were hard to rectify. Also in that moment she feared Mrs Turner would come in and not listen to the full story.

Perhaps the new housekeeper really had changed since Mr Sewell's illness but Emma was unconvinced. Mrs Turner would like an excuse to throw Emma out; if she saw she had the pocket watch she would take it as proof of Emma's guilt.

She jumped when the bell finally rang for someone to go to the small parlour but there was no time to quell the trembling in her legs before she ran up. She couldn't afford any delay — especially if she were going to ask that they allowed her to speak to them.

As she knocked softly and entered she regretted the position of the pocket watch in her clothes. It would be awkward to pull out while talking, yet the sight of it might encourage them to listen to the whole story. In the next second Emma was pleased it remained safe where it was because Mrs Turner was in the room too, standing in front of Her Ladyship and Miss Elizabeth. She was turned as far away from Mrs Honey as she could but there was no doubt she was standing in front of the seated former housekeeper as well.

Emma hurried over to pick up the tray. She'd write a note to Mrs Honey instead, she thought.

'Leave the tea things for now, Emma.'

She started. It was Her Ladyship's voice. She straightened up but remained where she was in front of the side tea table.

'Come and stand over here for a moment,' Her Ladyship went on.

Emma went to stand as far from Mrs Turner as possible and close to Mrs Honey. Mrs Honey gave her an encouraging smile.

'Emma, you know Mitchfield House,'

Her Ladyship said.

'I did spend some time there, Your Ladyship.' Emma cleared her throat because her voice came out much smaller than she'd intended.

Mrs Honey nodded, still smiling at her. What was this all about?

'What sort of estate is it?' Her Ladyship asked.

'It's a fine house,' Emma said, 'Not as large as the Hall. The grounds are not so extensive.'

'And the surroundings?'

'We only went to the nearby town, Your Ladyship. It was adequate for our provisions but . . . '

'But?' Her Ladyship pressed.

'There are no fine shops, Your Ladyship.'

'Did you learn anything of any estates nearby?'

'No. Mitchfield House seemed to be the largest in the surrounding area.'

'Splendid,' Her Ladyship said, unexpectedly. 'One could lead a secluded life there, then.'

Her Ladyship glanced at her daughter who was sitting back in her chair with one hand over her belly. Emma felt hot as she suddenly had an inkling of who might be wishing to lead a secluded life — at least for a while.

So the Earl was sending Miss Elizabeth to his new house instead of marrying her!

Emma turned to Her Ladyship. 'There is a lot of gossip in the town, Your Ladyship. People knew about us before we knew about them.'

Her Ladyship laughed, and so did Mrs Honey.

'I'm afraid that is the way of the world,' Her Ladyship said, looking at Emma appraisingly. 'But thank you for your honesty. If my daughter took over Mitchfield House, would you go with her?'

Emma's head was spinning. Lady's maid to Miss Elizabeth — or nursemaid afterwards because she knew the house and district?

'It would be a very small household

287

to begin with,' Her Ladyship went on. 'You may wish to come back here once the household grows.'

Not nursemaid then. What would her role be?

'But in the meantime you may pick your own staff. Elizabeth would like Kitty with her, if you could get the girl to agree.'

'Pick my staff?' Emma could almost feel Mrs Turner bristling beside her.

'Emma,' Mrs Honey said gently. She glanced at Her Ladyship, who nodded. 'Her Ladyship is asking you — temporarily — to be Housekeeper at Mitchfield House. You will need to quickly prepare the house for Miss Elizabeth to occupy and she will be joined by someone else shortly. They will live quietly for a year or so and then will decide whether to move elsewhere or remain. If they remain, they will begin to enter society again and the house will function much like this one, with entertaining and visitors. You may at that stage feel the job is too much for you and move on or come back here — in an enhanced role, of course. Or you may grow into the role at Mitchfield.'

Emma was speechless! Run the household of the odious Earl of Thorncombe? She could pick her staff! Here was a chance to do some good.

'Thank you, Mrs Honey,' Her Ladyship said. 'You've explained the situation more clearly than I could have. Do you need time to consider this, Emma? You have family nearby perhaps that you do not want to leave?'

Emma shook her head. 'On the contrary, Your Ladyship, my family are closer to Mitchfield House. But — would I be working for the Earl of Thorncombe?'

'No. His Lordship has taken over the lease of Mitchfield. You would be answerable to me.'

'Think about it, Emma,' Mrs Honey urged. 'Your own salary would increase and Miss Elizabeth wishes to offer a generous wage to the six or seven others you think would be hard-working, and above all discreet. Since townspeople love to gossip she cannot afford to take staff with her who like to spread gossip.'

'I understand, Mrs Honey,' Emma said.

'We will speak again tomorrow,' Her Ladyship said, and Emma was dismissed.

'Now, Turner,' Her Ladyship went on as Emma picked up the tray. 'I appreciate this leaves you with a servant problem but you understand that until Mr Hardcastle is able to join her we wish our daughter to have people she trusts . . . '

Emma closed the door.

They trusted her enough to make her housekeeper — even if only for a short while and of a small household. Emma didn't know what to think! She took the tea things to the scullery to begin to wash them when Kitty joined her.

'You were a long time,' she said. 'Oh, blow, there's Cook calling. She's in a flap because she's had to conjure up Her Ladyship's evening meal out of nothing.'

'I've a lot to tell you,' Emma said. 'Do you remember when Mr Hardcastle was here?'

'He's that attorney, isn't he? It was summer,' Kitty said. 'It was a particularly dry June and they spent all that time wandering around outside, do you remember? Eric kept seeing them.'

'Three months,' Emma mused as Kitty left.

If Kitty helped Miss Elizabeth with her bath and with dressing, she would know the truth and perhaps how far along Miss Elizabeth was. She'd need to convince Kitty to sit up with her and William that night. She had a feeling they would be talking until daylight.

23

Monica was back, Emma realised as she scurried round helping Cook with dinner. Monica was ensconced with Mrs Turner in the housekeeper's room for a very long time and even missed the light meal the servants had together after the family tea was over.

It was put down to Mr Sewell's illness that information of her arrival had not reached Cook and Her Ladyship was sympathetic. Soup, meat and vegetables and a fruit tart would suffice, she agreed. Her guest would be happy with that.

After the servants' meal, William hurried off to prepare the table and make sure the glasses and cutlery were polished. He worried about choosing the wine and wondered if he could go and ask Mr Sewell's advice.

'Choose what you think,' Emma

suggested, 'and take them to Mr Sewell for him to approve. I think he would like that.'

'Mr Sewell spoke to me!' William reported back afterwards. 'He's sitting up in bed, and he had some soup and bread and he nodded and said, 'Good choices'. It took him a long time to say and half of his face doesn't work, but still . . . '

'That's wonderful!' Emma said heartily. 'He must be on the mend.'

After the last course had been sent up and William was still upstairs serving and pouring the wine he'd chosen so successfully, and Cook was taking a breather, Emma was yet again up to her elbows in soapy water and thinking of Ada whose life this had been. If she could choose her own staff, would she be allowed to choose Ada to be cook and Jean and Connie to be housemaids? Kitty as Miss Elizabeth's lady's maid. And could she make the case that the gardens needed to be tidied so an under-gardener could be taken from the Hall? And one trusted footman, of course.

She hoped William wouldn't mind being left — he wouldn't want to go, she thought, with the sweet Flora to court.

As Emma's imagination ran riot she wondered if she could introduce a nursemaid later. Someone with her own child, admittedly, which may be problematic, but someone Miss Elizabeth could totally trust to be discreet. Emma was scared, she had to admit. It had all gone wrong when she'd got full of herself before. But there was so much potential for good for so many people, she didn't think she could pass the opportunity by.

Into these optimistic imaginings burst Monica and Mrs Turner together, both looking angry and dangerous.

'Where is it?' Monica said in a loud, rough voice. 'It's not in our room. What have you done with it?' She took hold of Emma's arm and spun her round to face them, then pushed her hard against the sink.

Emma gave a small cry and put her hand on her back where it had been pressed against the stone. Her heart, so full of possibilities before, was hammering. She didn't answer. Monica's angry face terrified her. This woman looked as though she was capable of anything.

'Get upstairs,' Monica said under her breath and to Emma the quiet voice was more menacing than the shouting. There was no one to see as the two women shoved Emma out into the passageway and up the stairs to the attic.

'All right, I'm going,' Emma said as strong hands pinched her upper arms and shoved her so she stumbled and hit her shin on the stairs. The rough treatment stopped for a moment when they reached her room. It had been turned upside down. Emma didn't have much but it had been tossed aside.

'Where is it?' Monica demanded again.

'I don't know what you mean,' Emma said, though she knew she wouldn't convince them.

'Liar!' Mrs Turner was standing with her arms folded. Most of the pushing and hitting had come from Monica but Mrs Turner was frightening too. 'You can't go around the village talking and not expect it to get back to the person you're talking about,' she went on.

Emma shivered at the coldness in her voice.

So the two ruffians had run to the Earl after all — but where was he for them to have got word to him so easily? Worse, Mrs Turner and Monica were still working for the Earl and he'd told them Emma had the pocket watch. So that was where Monica had been all day. But surely there hadn't been time for her to get to Thorncombe and back.

Without warning the older woman took hold of the top of Emma's apron and pulled it hard. Emma was jerked towards Mrs Turner and then fell back again as the material ripped. Mrs Turner then approached Emma and tore the cap from her head, then put her hands in Emma's hair feeling for anything hidden there. Emma cried out again as clumps of her hair were pulled out with the cap and she lifted her hands to protect her head. In that moment Mrs Turner tugged at her dress in the same way that she'd torn the apron off!

Emma looked down at herself, humiliated and despairing, in her torn underwear after the pocket watch had fallen out and Monica had pounced on it. If she could edge her way round Mrs Turner and out of the door, would there be time for her to run to the main part of the house before they caught up with her? If she could just talk to Mrs Honey this could still be sorted out. Did she dare run through the house in torn clothes?

Mrs Turner stood firmly in front of the door, her eyes on Emma. 'Get dressed and go,' Mrs Turner said threateningly. 'Take your things and leave.'

There wasn't much to pack. She put on her spare underwear and her day clothes and packed her few personal possessions.

Then Monica gripped her arm again. Emma was walked and pushed to the gate. It stood open, as it usually did, but she heard it clang shut behind her and the key turn.

There hadn't been a chance to go and hide in the folly to see William before she left.

It was dark. Every now and then the clouds covered the waning moon and it was no longer the bright, friendly, yellow moon she'd looked up at with Thomas. She was supposed to be sitting in the servants' hall telling William and Kitty about her eventful day and wonderful news. Instead she was standing alone and in pain on the road with no money and nowhere to go. When a nocturnal animal cried out, Emma screamed in alarm.

How had she gone in such a short space of time from optimism and hope for a better future to something far worse than anything that had gone before? From the thought that she could decide her own life to the certain knowledge that it was decided for her by others.

Emma put her shoulders back and lifted her chin. No, it wasn't like that. It would only be decided by others if she let them.

She walked quickly towards the village. The road up to the deserted house and the hills and forest beyond frightened her more than going this way. Perhaps Silas and his wife would take pity on her and let her sleep on their floor tonight. It would be hard to explain to them and they may lose sympathy with her once it became clear the pocket watch was lost again.

If not, she thought to make her way to the clearing where Mary Ann's cottage was. She could sleep in the forest and watch when it was light for a moment when Thomas was alone.

She heard a noise behind her, and thought the gate of the Hall had opened and a dark shape slipped out.

In a heart-stopping moment Emma thought William had come after her to say Her Ladyship wanted her to come back, but no one followed her. The shadow that came out hurried in the other direction. William would never think she'd go that way. The figure wasn't tall enough to be William anyway. She thought it had been her imagination.

She wouldn't show herself to Lily, she decided. Lily's secret would be safe if that was what she wanted, although Emma shed a tear that Lily would never know the picture she had conjured up, of Lily's child growing up playing in the grounds of Mitchfield House with Miss Elizabeth's child.

As if that could ever have been possible.

Surely Emma wasn't friendless. Thomas had nothing to give her and wasn't well enough to go with her, but perhaps Mary Ann could find her something to eat for her journey. For she'd have to go home, of course. Shamed and penniless as she was, they'd still take her in.

No, Emma wasn't alone. She just had to get through this night and the next two on the road and she'd be safe.

The inn was in darkness. That was strange. It wasn't so late and she'd imagined people would drink and be social into the night. Maybe not hard-working country people, who would have to rise early in the morning. Or maybe Silas had been afraid and not opened today. Emma was beginning to understand real fear. She pressed herself against the door of the inn as a dark horse cantered by carrying a dark-clad figure. This was the stuff of nightmares. The rider passed, on his way about his own business, Emma thought, whatever that was at this time of night.

Then as she was deciding whether to knock at the door or try to reach Mary Ann's cottage, the rider turned the horse and had it canter back. It came so close Emma thought she'd be crushed or trampled but the rider dismounted right in front of her. She looked away, but then gasped as the rider grasped her by the waist and swung her up on the horse, then mounted again behind her. She didn't have time to struggle.

The horse trotted back towards the Hall. It wasn't any of the horses from His Lordship's stable, Emma was sure, nor any of the grooms or stable boys. As they approached the Hall the rider slowed their mount to less than walking pace. Were they going to stop there or was he just trying to pass by as silently as possible?

His hands held her rather than the reins and there was no chance of Emma jumping down. She couldn't speak. Not even a *who are you?* If this man meant her no ill he would have spoken by now. Her breath came in rasping shallow gasps and she could only hear her own heartbeat in her ears. Her worst fears were confirmed when they trotted slowly past the firmly shut gates of the Hall and up towards the deserted house.

24

The house was further from the road than Emma had realised and harvest was over, so why would anyone even look towards the house that had stood there empty all these long years?

The rider dismounted and pulled her down, not minding that she fell to the ground. She struggled up, stiff and sore from the ride. Her captor was not much taller than her and he was fat, but he was strong. His arms had lifted her as easily as if she were a kitten.

The front door stood ajar and it looked as though the lock hadn't worked for a long time. Once inside, if she could escape she wouldn't have any problem getting out of the house. But it was such a long way to run to the village — unless she could hide in the forest. Emma thought she wouldn't have the courage but the only alternative was dying here — and her body never being found because no one would look for her here.

No groom came to take the horse to its stable. No footman came to greet them. The house smelled damp and dirty and was lit only by moonlight. A mattress had been dragged down and put in a corner of the entrance hall, and all the other doors stood shut. Perhaps this was the only sound space after so many years' neglect.

Her captor held her firmly by the wrist and didn't let go. She couldn't take her eyes off the makeshift bed where something glinted gold. And behind that wedged against the wall was a bundle of brown envelopes.

'Ah, I see you've noted my latest acquisition.' Her captor spoke and it was the voice she had expected, and feared, to hear. 'This may not be the setting you would expect to see me in but, as you see, I have good and faithful servants.'

Emma looked around wildly. Monica must have run up with the pocket watch the minute Emma left. Would she permit Emma to be murdered? Yes, and take part in the act, no doubt!

'If you think there is someone here to save you, you are sorely mistaken.' The Earl pulled Emma round to face him and she could feel his breath on her face. Then he pushed her away and she fell onto the mattress. 'Sadly,' he said, 'you are not a pretty little thing although with your tresses about you like that as if you have just got out of bed, it is some improvement.'

Emma shifted on the mattress so her feet were firmly on the ground and her hand brushed the pile of documents.

'Do not touch those,' he said, and his tone was unexpectedly conversational. 'That is my version of my father's Last Will and Testament and the deeds to the properties my poor long-dead mother didn't want me to have.' He laughed. 'You thought you could better me?'

'All I wanted was the pocket watch, but if it's so important to you, you can have it. Let me go home to my family and I'll tell no one.'

'Yes, it's important to me,' he said. 'Because Lewin looks at me with pity and thinks he's so much better than me.' He looked around the room. 'This is just for now. I have more wealth and property than you or he can imagine.'

'I believe you, sir,' Emma said. 'But you won't risk losing it by killing an insignificant servant. I'll go tonight and not speak a word.'

He walked away and Emma was sure he was looking for something to kill her with without delay.

There was a sound from outside. She thought it was voices but in her terror she realised it was only the wind, because the Earl took no notice.

Summoning courage she never knew she had, she closed her hand around the pocket watch and leapt up from the mattress, pushing him as hard as she could. He stumbled with the unexpectedness of the shove, letting out a curse. Once he was on his face on the floor

Emma took her chance.

She would head towards the forest and hills, she decided. He would never expect that and so long as he didn't see her he would stumble or ride in the other direction.

She tore the door wide open and ran.

It took him a few moments to get up from the floor, hampered by his age and size and, she hoped, the shock of her attack. She sped as fast as she could headlong down the path to the gate and turned immediately left.

There was that sound again, now behind her. Surely it was too soon for him to have reached the gate as well. Someone called her name and she felt a figure beside her. He was so much faster than she had expected.

She looked around. Behind her, about to go up the path to the house, were a dozen men carrying what looked like stout sticks. And beside her, ready to catch her when she fell, was Thomas.

★ ★ ★

Once again Emma was seated on a horse in front of a rider and with strong arms around her — but, oh, how different was this experience.

She was draped in a rough jacket that she thought looked like William's, but someone had surrendered it gladly to warm her and Thomas held her fast against him for her comfort and safety. She leaned back gratefully.

'How did you know where I was?' she asked.

'I saw him take you and head in this direction. The villagers have suspected he was here.'

'Why are the villagers here with you?'

'When I told Mary Ann what had happened she flew up and down the road knocking on doors for help. She knew who the rider was and half the village would like to see him brought to justice.'

They reached the Hall where the gate now stood open. Thomas turned the horse to the house.

'I can't go back here,' Emma said in

alarm. 'I've been dismissed and Monica and Mrs Turner mean me harm!'

'Did you not see, Emma? William ran back up to the Hall once he knew you were safe. The villagers are going to take the Earl to the magistrates and Monica and Mrs Turner will be turned over to the authorities too. Mrs Honey is waiting for you.'

'How did the people at the Hall know? How did William come to be up at the deserted house?'

'Emma, don't be angry with me for keeping a secret from you. Lily is living at Mary Ann's and she ran to the Hall to tell them.'

'I knew it, Thomas. But she wanted it to be a secret from all of us.'

'She gladly surrendered her secret to help you.'

'She left the baby behind?' Emma asked.

'She took her daughter in her arms and ran. William reported that when he left to come to help you she was being passed from hand to hand in the servants' parlour and Mrs Honey had offered to make hot chocolate for everyone! I don't know if I misunderstood or not that Her Ladyship and Miss Elizabeth were there as well. I think Lily probably knocked rather loudly at the door!'

'Oh, Thomas. I have to see this!' Emma said.

★　★　★

The baby was a dear little thing and the chocolate tasted good, but Emma was so very tired. It had been an extraordinarily long day. It was Miss Elizabeth who said that Emma should be put to bed. Dead on her feet, she still took a moment to say goodnight to Thomas.

She opened her mouth to ask a question but he kissed it instead. 'We have the rest of our lives to talk,' he said. 'Sleep now.'

She nodded. 'I love you, Thomas.'

He bent to kiss her brow. 'I love you, Emma.'

It was Mrs Honey who accompanied her.

'It's the wrong stairs,' she said as the former housekeeper guided Emma up the main staircase.

'You shall have my room, Emma.'

There was a small bed in the best guest room as well as the big high bed for important guests and with Mrs Honey in the small bed in a corner of the room, she knew she could sleep easy. She lay on the bed, too exhausted to do anything else, and Mrs Honey drew a cover over her.

Only then did she relinquish what was in her hand. 'Can you give this to Mr Sewell, please, Mrs Honey?'

Mrs Honey took the precious object carefully.

'His Lordship will be back soon,' she said. 'But I shall make sure Mr Sewell sees it on the way back to its rightful owner.'

It had been a roundabout way to get the pocket watch back to His Lordship but she'd done it — and solved two mysteries in the process.

25

Thomas delivered her to the door of Mary Ann's cottage and left. Mary Ann settled them both in the most comfortable chairs and served them with herbal drinks and little cakes and then disappeared herself.

Now it was just the two of them and they were finally able to talk for the first time in five months.

'I'm sorry I didn't tell you where I was,' Lily said.

'I understand, Lily,' Emma said. 'You had your reputation to think of. Or at least Mrs Honey thought of it for you — I had a long talk with her.'

'I know you would never betray my secret,' Lily said. 'But Mrs Honey entreated me not to tell you.'

'Mrs Honey kept in touch with you all this time?'

Lily nodded. 'She's been better than

a mother.' Lily's eyes filled with tears. 'She found me a place with Mary Ann and brings money every month.'

'It was the Earl of Thorncombe, wasn't it?'

'Yes.' Lily reached out to touch Emma's arm. 'William said you've been worried about me.' She looked away as if wondering how best to explain herself, then looked Emma in the eyes. 'It was a foolish thing, Emma. I know it was wrong and it was only the once. I don't harbour any desire for him now but he was wretched — sad that his mother had never liked him and miserable because his father had died.'

There was a rustling in the crib by her feet as the Earl's daughter made her presence felt.

'But once was enough,' Emma said. 'Have you grown to love her?' she asked as Lily picked the child up and nestled her close.

'Mary Ann convinced me she was all mine and none of his,' Lily said. 'I had a moment of doubt when she was first born because she looked so much like him.' She laughed. 'But, you know, he's not a bad-looking man.' Lily adjusted the position of the baby. 'I hope you don't mind, Emma,' she said. 'I've called her after you.'

Emma gasped. 'Her name's Emma?'

'I haven't been able to take her to the church, but Mary Ann and I held a little ritual in the woods. We named her — before God and the trees and the whole of nature — Emma Mary, because Mary Ann is wonderful too. I thought if she grew to be half as good and brave and clever as you, she would go on all right.'

'How was it when you took her to the Hall the night before last?' Emma asked, her voice choked with emotion.

'William opened the door to me and fortunately understood the situation quickly,' Lily said. 'I was so surprised to see Mrs Honey! I thought I must be dreaming the whole thing!'

'I was feeling that at the same time,'

Emma said, now able to laugh about her experience.

'I can imagine so. Mrs Honey took the baby and I ran to wake the outdoor staff while William hurried up to the deserted house.'

'And Mary Ann woke the villagers,' Emma said. 'I feel so grateful.'

'The villagers are grateful to *you*,' Lily said. 'The Earl had control in this village for too long.'

'But such gratitude is not warranted,' Emma said. 'It was you and Mary Ann, the villagers and Hall staff who brought about the Earl's capture.'

'And his wife and her mother,' Lily said.

Emma froze. 'What?'

'Oh,' Lily said. 'Did you not realise? The Earl of Thorncombe was good at exercising power but Mrs Turner was better and managed to arrange a secret wedding between him and her daughter.'

'I thought they could be mother and daughter,' Emma said. 'I believed I saw someone come out of the gate after me and go in that direction. I'm guessing it was Monica running the pocket watch up to the Earl in the deserted house. But he called her his servant.'

Lily laughed. 'It may have suited him to say so, but Mrs Turner ruled in that household much more than in Lord Lewin's.'

When she recovered from her surprise, Emma had another question. 'Mary Ann said the parish constable — or the person he chose to act for him — was a tool of the Earl as well.'

'The villagers took them straight to the magistrates without telling the constable. They are in prison and we hope he doesn't have any power over the magistrates.' Lily thought for a moment. 'Apparently Mrs Turner has a sister as scheming as she is. The fear is that she will contrive to free them, but we can hope he's learned his lesson and at least won't return here.'

'I may have met the sister,' Emma said. 'I think she came to Mitchfield

House. Was it her brother she came with or her husband?'

'Her husband, according to what Mary Ann knows from the villagers, is as much under her control as the Earl is under Mrs Turner's.'

'I'm surprised the Earl would marry Monica,' Emma said. 'When he could have had someone like Miss Elizabeth.' Emma thought for a moment. 'Monica doesn't have a child, does she?'

'No, but Mary Ann believes Mrs Turner could have convinced him there was one. The Earl fell so low since I knew him. She tricked him when he was vulnerable.' Lily considered for a moment, then laughed. 'Sometimes I'm glad not to have any family but you and Mary Ann and Mrs Honey.'

'I'm so glad to see you happy, Lily,' Emma said heartily. 'Will you be able to stay here?'

'Mary Ann says so.' Lily nodded. 'Whether that's best for Emma Mary as she grows up, I don't know. And Mary Ann may long for her peace and quiet again as she gets more active. I could pretend to be a widow and get a place, but I don't want to be parted from my daughter.'

The nightmare would not be so easily forgotten but Thomas was waiting for Emma back at Lewin Hall and the choices she was going to be able to make for the future were beginning to take shape.

*   *   *

The Journal, 18th February, 1845
  Edgar the 8th Earl of Thorncombe died at Oxford on the 13th inst. aged 47. He lived a controversial life with rumours around him of significant gambling debts and of involvement in various criminal activities, none proven. He narrowly avoided imprisonment last September, along with his wife and his wife's mother, when no concrete evidence of thefts from Lewin Hall and other properties could be produced. The mystery of the robbery at the Hall

was never solved.

The Earl is survived by his wife, who continues to live quietly in Thorncombe village with her mother and her aunt and uncle.

Thorncombe Manor, with debts still pending from extensive repairs carried out by the 8th Earl, passes to the nephew of the 7th Earl who resides abroad and has yet to take possession of the crumbling property.

26

The bridal party left from Mitchfield House but after the ceremony, the destination was the bride and groom's cottage. April, 1846 had been wet but May had been hot and dry, so the wedding guests were hopeful of holding the party outside.

With her ring on her finger and Thomas beside her driving the grey horse home, Emma laughed with happiness. In her new lavender cotton dress she could almost believe it when people told her she was beautiful. She leaned her head against Thomas's shoulder, careful not to crush the flowers in her hair, and listened to their families in the cart and their friends walking beside them.

'The service was lovely,' Emma's mother said, trying to contain the wriggling toddler who had been allowed to ride in the cart with them.

'A bit different to the last wedding we went to there, eh, Emma?' Jean called to her.

It was true. Miss Elizabeth hadn't had many guests and the bells hadn't pealed. But later the new Mrs Hardcastle had congratulated Ada for the eight-course meal and Emma for the flawless service and excellent running of the household. The couple and their child were ready to return to a society where no one knew the wedding date.

Emma looked forward to running a cottage for two rather than a big house, and had plans to grow herbs and learn to make soaps and lotions. They were lucky that the cottage the farmer had given them had a good plot of land for planting. Thomas had flourished working the land.

'Do you want me to take Emma Mary?' Lily called to the women in the cart.

'She's all right,' Emma's mother answered.

Thomas's mother added, 'I heard the

Queen was safely delivered of her child last week.'

'Her fourth, isn't it?' Jean called, laughing.

'No, her fifth,' Thomas's mother explained, not understanding the reference to the drunken housekeeper who had toasted the last birth a year and a half earlier at Mitchfield.

Emma turned to touch her mother-in-law on the shoulder. 'When we arrive I'll tell you the story of the first housekeeper of Mitchfield House.'

She remained with her hand on the other woman's shoulder as they passed the cottage that would soon be Ada and Jimmy's.

When Ada left service the hope was she and Emma would open a tea shop, still sadly lacking in the town. Well, their partners had been enterprising, operating a transport business with the backing of the farmer, who also made a profit, so why shouldn't they?

'I saw that Thomas dropped the ring in the church,' his mother commented.

'Was it because you were nervous or did someone tell you it was good luck to do that?'

'It is good luck,' Emma's mother agreed. 'I was pleased he did.'

Thomas looked down at Emma beside him and she felt as though her heart would stop with the intensity of the love in that look.

'It was nerves,' he whispered. 'We don't need gestures like that to bring us luck, do we?'

She turned her face up to kiss his lips.

'No,' she agreed heartily. 'We make our own good fortune.'

We do hope that you have enjoyed reading this large print book.

Did you know that all of our titles are available for purchase?

We publish a wide range of high quality large print books including:
Romances, Mysteries, Classics General Fiction Non Fiction and Westerns

Special interest titles available in large print are:
The Little Oxford Dictionary Music Book, Song Book Hymn Book, Service Book

Also available from us courtesy of Oxford University Press:
Young Readers' Dictionary (large print edition) Young Readers' Thesaurus (large print edition)

For further information or a free brochure, please contact us at:
**Ulverscroft Large Print Books Ltd., The Green, Bradgate Road, Anstey, Leicester, LE7 7FU, England.
Tel:** (00 44) **0116 236 4325
Fax:** (00 44) **0116 234 0205**

WILD SPIRIT

Dawn Knox

It's Rae's dream to sail away across oceans on her family's boat, the *Wild Spirit* — but in 1939 the world is once again plunged into conflict, and her travel plans must be postponed. When Hitler's forces trap the Allies on the beaches of Dunkirk, Rae sails with a fleet of volunteer ships to attempt the impossible and rescue the desperate servicemen. However, her bravery places more lives than her own in jeopardy — including that of Jamie MacKenzie, the man she's known and loved for years . . .

RETURN TO TASMANIA

Alan C. Williams

Heading back from Sydney to her idyllic childhood home in Tasmania, Sandie's priorities are to recover from a bullet wound, reconsider her future in the police, and spend time with her sister and niece. But even as the plane lands, she senses that a fellow passenger is not all he seems. When a series of suspicious events follow her arrival, the mystery man reveals himself as Adam, who has been sent to protect Sandie's family as they become embroiled in the fall-out following the double-crossing of a dangerous criminal.

THE ENGLISH AU PAIR

Chrissie Loveday

Stella Lazenby flies to Spain to work as an au pair for Isabel and Ignacio Mendoza, looking after their sons Juan and Javier. The parents are charming, the boys delightful — and then there's the handsome Stefano, who becomes more than a friend . . . But all is not as perfect as it seems. Housekeeper Maria resents Stella's presence, and Isabel worries that her husband is hiding secrets. Then Stefano is accused of stealing from Ignacio's company, and Stella doesn't know what to believe . . .

DANGER FOR DAISY

Francesca Capaldi

Mature student Daisy Morgan plucks up her courage to attend a get-together — only to cannon straight into a handsome gentleman, spilling her drink all over his smart suit into the bargain! To make matters worse, he turns out to be Seth, her flatmates' archaeologist friend. After this unconventional meeting, sparks quickly kindle between the pair, and Daisy accompanies Seth to a dig on a remote island. But danger lurks on Sealfarne — and they are about to unearth it . . .

THE BRIDE IS MISSING

Anne Hewland

Cat is meant to be marrying Stephen after a whirlwind romance. So why is she now waking up on a small Welsh island, still in her hen party outfit? She initially thinks it's a pre-wedding prank — but soon it becomes apparent that the reality is much more sinister. Along with Greg, the man who discovered her when she woke by the beach, Cat is drawn into the web of intrigue which has entangled both her fiancé and her best friend . . .